AMID MORTAL WORDS

WE STAND BETWEEN THE LIVING AND THE DEAD

ROBERT CHAZZ CHUTE

EX PARTE PRESS

PRAISE FOR ROBERT'S WORK

Chute sucks you in from word one and pulls you down his post apocalyptic rabbit hole! You will sleep with the lights on, covers pulled over your head and dust off the old teddy bear for comfort. Horrifically well written and engaging. There are other popular books in this genre, but after reading this there is nothing else that climbs to the heights of Chute's caliber. Chazz ranks among the top tier of our generation's storytellers. ~ Alex Kimmell, Author of *The Key to Everything*

Robert Chazz Chute is such a skilled spinner of tales that the reader is more than willing to suspend any possible disbelief to go along for the ride. ~ David Pandolfe, author of *Jump When Ready*

It's not very often one finds a writer with such a dark side that has such a great sense of humor. ~ Glenn Roberts, Amazon reviewer

The author has a definite talent with words and ideas. ~ Love to Read!, Amazon reviewer

His words lift and dance off the page, bringing the story to life. ~ Kindle Customer, Amazon reviewer

The world building is horrifically well done with twists and turns and deceit around every corner. ~ Wanda, Amazon reviewer

Nothing but sheer exhaustion could tear my eyes from the captivating dance of words choreographed by Robert Chazz Chute. ~ Halph Staph, Amazon reviewer

Wonderful action constantly holds your interest. ~ Sharon Finn, Amazon reviewer

The complexity and attention to detail throughout absolutely blows me away. ~ Kindle customer, Amazon Reviewer

Very few authors impress me with their actual writing style, it's usually always about the story. But this author paints such beautiful vivid pictures with words that I found myself not only enjoying the story but enjoying the way the words created images in my mind. I know that sounds corny, but it is true. ~ B.H., Amazon reviewer

Chute gives us story worthy of Stephen King. A read both thoughtful and fun. ~ Linda Beer Johnson, Amazon reviewer

The author does an excellent job building the characters and getting you invested and involved. ~ Michele L. Hebert, Amazon reviewer

I just can't say in words what a powerful author this is! ~ Delinda L. Calkins, Amazon reviewer

Robert Chazz Chute writes so skillfully as to make the supernatural seem perfectly logical - and terrifying! There are twists, turns and surprises galore. You will be glad you bought this book - until you lose sleep because you can't put it down. ~ johligo, Amazon reviewer

When I want to read apocalyptic books or zombie stories, those books have to also be extremely well-written and something that I could recommend with zeal and confidence to everyone I know. Robert Chazz Chute's books are exactly that. ~ Mazie Lane, Amazon reviewer

He makes the stuff that is obviously fiction, believable. ~ W. Nickels, Amazon reviewer

I am a lover of paranormal, dystopian novels and depth of story as well as intelligence in writing style, and Robert has it all. Humor, wit, depth, intelligence and an awesome way with words/writing. ~ Amazon Customer, Amazon reviewer

LICENSE NOTES

AMID MORTAL WORDS
We Stand Between the Living and the Dead
Robert Chazz Chute

Published by Ex Parte Press
Copyright © 2019 Robert Chazz Chute
ISBN (paperback): 978-1-927607-60-2
ISBN (ebook): 978-1-927607-61-9

AUTHOR'S NOTE

If you could punish all the bad people and make them disappear, would you? What would the world look like if you did? We all have revenge fantasies. If you acted on those fantasies, would you be the hero or the villain? *Amid Mortal Words* starts from that premise.

After completing the *AFTER Life* trilogy and *All Empires Fall* in 2018, I didn't think I would write another apocalyptic novel so soon. I had just released *The Night Man* and thought some more crime fiction was in order. However, the muse wants what the muse wants. The ideas and twists for this book hit me between the eyes repeatedly, usually at four in the morning. This story literally would not allow me to sleep. Sometimes when writing is going well it feels a little like taking dictation. Sometimes it washes over you like an undeniable fever and the only way to stop the pestering is to write it all down.

I hope you enjoy *Amid Mortal Words*. If you dig what I sling, please leave a brief review wherever you purchased this book. You will find more apocalyptic tales in the listings at the end of this book.

Thanks and all the best!
Robert

PART I

THE ENGINEERING PROBLEM

And God said,
"Let there be Right!"
There was Right
and it was good.
On the sixth day,
He introduced the Wrong
that would doom the project.

And the four angels, who had been prepared for the hour and day and month and year, were released, so that they would kill a third of mankind. ~ Revelation 9:15

IN THE BEGINNING

They threw themselves from burning towers. Far off, I heard screams of pain but none cried out for mercy. They were sure no help would come. Wandering through shock and a fog of embers, I stumbled amid the ruins of What Was. Only I knew how this began, how the plan unfolded and how I'd failed to stop it.

All my life I had assumed safety was, if not assured, fairly likely. I ignored the truth: A life can end at any moment. A complete nuclear exchange, beginning to end, lasts thirty minutes at the outside. After that, the math of extinction is merciless. Add up all the minuses and eventually Earth's human population reaches zero, no remainders. I'd lived with the threat so long, I'd normalized the fear until I was numb to adrenaline's taste. I'd taken the efficiency of our weapons for granted. Only now did I truly understand how precarious survival really was.

Stumbling down a filthy alley, the same colorful graffiti greeted me on every wall that still stood: *The code is cracked! Your brain's been hacked!*

The dead, whether suicides or homicides or the victims of geno-cide, lay everywhere. Some corpses lay in piles and had become grim puzzles. Where did one body begin and another end? Caught in the first flash, some bodies had turned to ash at the feet of what had once been human silhouettes. I covered my mouth and nose with a piece of cloth so I would not inhale the ashes and stink of the fallen. Feverish and weak, I fought to keep down my gorge as I stumbled on through the gray twilight. It should have been midday but rising smoke and roiling black clouds choked the sunlight as the world burned. I felt like I was slowly suffocating.

At the base of a high-rise, I looked up in awe. A shock wave had shattered all the glass of a skyscraper and only the building's bones were left, picked clean, bent and broken. I looked down to wipe tears and grit from my eyes. That's where I came upon the book again.

The paperback's pages fluttered in the hot breath of the poisoned wind. Something irresistible caught my eye among its pages. I bent to read a note scribbled in the margins. The handwriting was a slanted slash that made me think of cut throats.

THE BEGINNING and end of anything starts with a train of thought. Nothing just happens. There are always causes. Reason the why.

THE NEXT PAGE was torn out and there was no more to work with.

I wondered, *This is the why of what? How much more was there to the message? What was the beginning of the world's end?*

Too many questions, not enough answers. I tried to think of other things but found I could not. Thoughts are connections. My connections were broken. My mind had become a labyrinth and at every turn I found yet another locked door.

How did I get here?

I straightened to heave my heavy pack, to readjust the thick straps and shift its weight on my aching shoulders. That's when I noticed one pocket had been cut. I struggled to remember what was in that pocket. A can of soup, perhaps? Back in the fearful huddle of the crowded tunnels beneath the streets, I'd felt like a trapped rat.

We thought we'd starve down there (but not, perhaps, before eating each other).

The soup thief had not yet read from the book nor heard my message. No matter. If the message found them first, they would receive swift justice by their own hand. If the message did not worm its way into the criminal's brain, radiation would do the job. Radiation is not so merciful. That way out is like swirling down a drain, exiting life through a pipe lined with razors.

In the distance, the echoing cries of despair tapered off. Of those who remained among the damned, the shrieks of pain sounded nearer. Thunder clapped as the sky opened up in a torrent of tainted rain, washing the ashes from the Earth. Experts said that it would take five years to cleanse the waste made by our worst weapons. I knew the projections all too well. I was one of those experts. What we didn't tell the public was that nuclear famine would end humanity long before that. I harbored no hope or fantasy that my species would survive to rise from the rubble. No matter how deep and fortified the bunker, our species' arc was done. Fast or slow, extinction's axe blade would fall upon everyone's neck.

I covered my ears, pressing my gloved palms hard against the sides of my head. Still, the sky rumbled ever louder until the thunderous percussion reverberated through my chest to rock my pounding heart. The end was undeniable. I sighed and stepped out from cover to surrender to the cooling, killing rain.

"We've been lied to," I said. "We were told the purge would strengthen us. They said that which does not kill us makes us stronger. I didn't realize how weak we really were before I got on that train to Chicago."

The storm raged but I knew lightning's retribution would not find me. I was condemned to witness the conflagration, somehow inside and outside reality at the same time. This nightmare was not of my creation but I had shared it. No one escaped the infection of a mind virus.

I AWOKE on a freezing cold metal table, naked and surrounded by unfamiliar medical devices. I found I could not scream. A tube snaked down my throat. Was the apocalypse I'd witnessed the future or the past? Someone, for reasons unknown, conspired to save me.

Though my invisible savior might have meant well, I was sure I would die from the fallout, slipping slowly, spiraling down the razor drain. Before I passed out, I prayed for the first time since I was a little boy. *Please don't let me fall. Don't let me fail.*

To my surprise, a voice replied to my unspoken thought. "Failure or success is entirely in your hands."

I don't understand!

"You will. Begin at the beginning. Start again. Forge a better fate."

2

THE TRAIN OF THOUGHT

I was startled awake from a nightmare and, for a moment, I wasn't sure where I was. All the details evaporated as soon as I swam back to consciousness but I shivered as if I had been on my back in a snowbank. Chills ran through me and then the cold sweat hit. My eyelids felt as if they'd been glued shut. I forced myself to peel one eye for a quick peek.

Ah, the train, I thought. *I'm headed east, safe, or as safe as anyone ever is on Amtrak.*

I waited for my racing heartbeat to slow. Out of the cool mountain air I craved, the train car's atmosphere felt stale. Even though the heat of the day was behind us as well, lazy fans did little to tame July's heat. The warm miasma of strangers' breath and sweat folded over me like a blanket. At least the chills subsided. I shifted in my seat uncomfortably.

I forced myself to open both eyes. The upholstery of the seat in front of me was old and stained with faint outlines, mysterious leavings from previous travelers. I noticed patterns within those stains. This one looked like an outline of a hand with eight fingers. That one looked like a person with one large eye that stared at me from beneath a crown of thorns.

Before I could squeeze my eyes shut again, I sensed I was no longer traveling alone.

Though my car on the California Zephyr was fairly empty, a stranger had plunked himself in the seat beside me. I risked a quick glance. A tall, thin man in an ill-fitting black suit sat in the next seat, apparently engrossed in a paperback. He might have been a tired forty or a well-preserved sixty.

The headache I'd left the Cheyenne Mountain Complex to escape was back. Not wishing to invite conversation, I retreated and leaned my left temple against the window to feel the cool pane of glass against my skin. I listened to the rattle and light percussive rhythms of the train as it ate rails and shat miles.

Charging through the big empty of the Midwest's darkness, I guessed the hour was late but it must soon become early. I had no idea how much longer I would have to mimic unconsciousness as we were carried through the night toward dawn. Pretending to fall back asleep soon felt silly. I was not a child and besides, the unknown is an itch.

As I pretended to rouse, I rubbed my eyes and looked at my new traveling companion. The thin man did not look up right away. He held a gold calligraphy pen and used it to scratch something in the back of his book. His hand covered the title but I got a glimpse of the author's name. I did not recognize it nor could I remember it a moment after taking it in.

My seatmate was a hawk-faced man with prominent brows and beady eyes. Though tall, he hunched forward from the shoulders as if he was trying to pull himself into the book.

"You're awake," he said. "Good morning."

"Good morning," I replied warily. "When did you get on the train?"

"Some time ago," he said vaguely. "You seem a deep sleeper. I hope I haven't disturbed you."

"Not at all."

"You've been sleeping a long time, traveling a long time." It seemed like more of a statement than a question.

"Since Denver," I lied.

"What's the last stop you remember?"

That struck me as an odd question. I wasn't sure.

The last thing I remembered was General Pitmore's aide, Lt. Megan Havelston, coming into my office after a budget allocation meeting. My head was throbbing and I was already in a bad mood when she asked if she had permission to speak freely.

I was surprised by her request. That expression is common in movies but it's not really a thing, especially in my work environment. "What's this about, Lieutenant?"

"General Pitmore is concerned you don't play pool or poker, sir."

"You are kidding me, right?"

"The General is concerned that you are too antisocial, sir."

"Not true. I'm asocial. Also, I wasn't aware I had to play nice to get the job done."

"But you are familiar with the term, 'team player,' sir."

"Don't lawyer me, Lieutenant. What's this about?"

"When General Pitmore is annoyed with a staff member, I notice he asks about heritage."

"Better send that signal again," I said.

"He asked about your name, if you're Mexican, sir."

"I don't see what that has to do with anything."

"He's worried about your loyalty, sir."

"If he's that sensitive about who is from where, all the Canadians on base are going to be awfully disappointed."

"Yes, sir, but it is what it is."

"I'm not much into genealogy, Lieutenant, but my last name is Salvador. It's Spanish. My family has been in this country for five generations. I wonder if that's more or fewer years than the Pitmores can claim as Americans."

Havelston, much wiser than her years, looked at me with something like pity.

"For the General, disagreement is disloyalty, sir. He's begun looking for excuses to lose you. Colonel Jeffries isn't the kind to disagree or defend you."

My immediate superior, Adam Jeffries, was working at Peterson

Air Force Base instead of in Cheyenne Mountain with me. I suspected the Colonel didn't enjoy being in the General's presence any more than I did. For the first time, I wondered if I'd been too naive about office politics. Maybe I'd been made General Pitmore's punching bag on purpose. I supposed that with a white-bread name like Jeffries, the Colonel had little to fear in losing his position.

My headache grew in size and power. I could feel a new wave of pain crashing behind my right eye. "So, Lieutenant ... you're saying, I have to do what, exactly?"

"Schmooze General Pitmore, sir. Be more social. He likes compliments."

"Thank you, Lieutenant, I'll take that under advisement. What's the worst that could happen? Reassignment to liaise with the NSA? I happen to like Maryland."

"It wouldn't be that. With all due respect, you're close to losing your job, sir. To quote the General, 'Lt. Col. Zane Salvador is on a glide path to a listening post in northernmost Alaska.'"

Her revelation genuinely startled me. I didn't care for my superiors but I didn't think I'd allowed them to see my disdain. I didn't agree with their hawkish stances, misplaced priorities and resistance to change. Stress headaches pounded through my skull like a drum when I had extended meetings, particularly when I had to deal with Pitmore.

Megan Havelston was one of the few staffers with whom I was friendly, an excellent officer who did her job well. Only because of our mutual respect did she dare approach me about the precarious status of my career. Relations with my superiors had fallen farther apart than I'd thought. I'd also assumed I was too valuable to national defense to be put on a shelf at a listening post in Alaska.

Havelston must have read the surprise on my face. "I'm sorry, sir."

"Did Pitmore or Jeffries send you here to warn me?"

"No, sir, but I'm wondering if a break from routine would help."

"Me?"

"You and our superiors, sir. You've been complaining about headaches — "

"I didn't complain," I said. "I mentioned them." As soon as it was out of my mouth I heard how defensive I sounded.

"Have you considered a medical leave to get some space? A cooling off period between you and the General? Maybe a little time away would give you both some perspective, sir."

"Is this General Pitmore's way of pushing me out? Irritating me into resigning?"

She took a deep breath. "I'm not trying to deceive you if that's what you're implying. I want you to keep your job, sir."

"Why?"

"Because I think you're one of the voices of reason around here."

"I like to think so. Very well. That will be sufficient, Lieutenant. You're dismissed."

I caught the look on her face before she turned for the door and regretted my tone. She was trying to help me. Her hand was on the doorknob when I called her back. If disagreement was disloyalty in Pitmore's eyes then the lieutenant had just risked her career to give me a chance at keeping my position. "Megan? Please inform the General that I have some leave coming up and I'd like to take it as soon as possible. I'll check in with the base doctor this afternoon, as well. And thank you, Lieutenant. I do appreciate your input."

I was out of Cheyenne Mountain the next day. I left my apartment in Briartown the day after that. The doctor had offered me pills and I refused, preferring instead to take a week off first, get more exercise and see a couple of old friends. I hoped the stress headaches would ease with conservative treatment. If time off and Tylenol didn't do the trick, I conceded to the base doctor that more medical investigation might be required.

The thin man was staring at me. What had he asked? "What's the last stop you remember?"

My last memory of Colorado Springs was standing in my bedroom with my suitcase open on the bed. I had been packing to finally get back East. An Amtrak digital ticket was downloaded to my phone and ....

After that, I drew a disturbing blank. Searching my memory for the trip to the train was like going to a kitchen cabinet to grab a coffee mug and finding the shelf empty. This wasn't merely like tip-of-the-tongue syndrome, searching for a missing word or a name.

Lost time, I thought. *Maybe it isn't just a headache. Maybe it's a brain tumor.*

3

WORD PHYSICS OF THE GRIMOIRE

"Pardon me," my new traveling companion said. "Where are my manners?" He offered his hand and I found that his large hand was soft and surprisingly cold. It was as if his veins were filled with ice. As we shook, he told me his name. Working on automatic, I told him mine. However, distracted by the frigid shock that raced up my arm, I instantly forgot the man's name.

As I rose through the ranks of the Air Force, a superior once taught me a trick to remember names at cocktail parties. "To set a memory in concrete, repeat the name the instant it is spoken and attach that name to some unique feature of the person."

That kindly officer was long since dead and though I could picture his face, I could no longer recall his first name with certainty. Memory is tricky. Sometimes the mind makes stuff up to fill in the gaps. Sometimes it blocks or erases what really happened. Often, the brain will fire up a tired neuron if you give it something else to think about. I'd been under a lot of pressure lately. I didn't care to remember anything about work. That's the purpose of stress leave.

As if the stranger could read my mind and decided to torture me, he asked what I did for a living. I was not accustomed to that question. Living in Colorado Springs, my uniform was the cardinal sign of what I might be up to at Cheyenne Mountain and most residents knew not to bother to ask for details. "I'm in Loss Prevention," I said.

"Ah. I'm in the dirty end of accounting," my seatmate volunteered. "Procurement."

"Nice." I had no idea what he meant by "the dirty end of accounting" and "nice" is what people say when there's little to be said. Eager to change the subject, I asked how he was enjoying his book.

"Sort of a thriller with lots of suspense. I don't know how I feel about it yet. It's quite enigmatic so far: unreliable narrator with some fine turns of phrase. I'm curious to find out where it ends up." The hawk-faced man pointed to the book that sat forgotten in my lap. "I see you're a reader, too."

"The wi-fi signal on these trains sucks so a paperback helps the clock spin," I said. "The views from the train through the mountains are amazing but once we're away from the mountains and the sun goes down and the butt goes numb … you know."

"Diving into a book can be a lovely distraction or an experience that swallows you." He craned his neck to look at the title. "Another end-of-the-world story? Those seem to be everywhere, don't they?"

"I don't find this one very realistic. I know how the world will end," I said.

He looked genuinely intrigued. "Do tell."

"There won't be any zombies or vampires."

He laughed. "I agree but you seem to have some special knowledge. How do you think the world will end precisely?"

"Like it started: in flames."

"Why do you think that?"

"Physics," I replied, "and if not because of physics, I like the symmetry of the narrative loop. Like they say, history repeats or rhymes."

My new companion looked puzzled.

"I read a lot of fiction," I explained.

"The mark of the lonely person."

"The sign of a contented one," I countered. "Anyway, in most good books, there's some kind of callback to the first chapter when you get to the end. Either way, I suspect the end is coming fast."

"Only if reality follows the narrative arc of a good book," he said. "I think events are more messy and difficult to predict than that. Do you really think we're near the end of the human story?"

I was more familiar with this question than the average person. Knowing the math was part of my job. "Have you ever heard of the German tank problem?"

"No, but I imagine German tanks posed quite a problem for their enemies."

"The German tank problem was an issue for mathematicians. Before the Normandy invasion, the Allies needed to estimate how many tanks they were likely to face. Using serial numbers from captured enemy tanks, Allied math whizzes extrapolated to figure it out. The statistical analysis turned out to be quite precise, even better when they figured out how many V-2 rockets were in production."

"I'm sorry, I don't follow."

"Bayes' theorem, Bayesian inference…the model is all about figuring out probabilities with very little data to go on. Doesn't matter. The math says humanity has somewhere between 20 and maybe 760 years left to exist, depending if you think we're closer to the beginning or end of our story."

"Doesn't matter? Ooh, I find this fascinating: 760 years? Really?"

"At the outside. People tend to think that's a long time but the most optimistic estimate suggests we are less than eight healthy generations away from the end of the world."

"At the outside?"

I bobbed my aching head. "Much less is more likely, I think."

"Why do you say that?"

"Because I watch videos on YouTube where people stack up rickety chairs to hang Christmas decorations."

"And that does not end well."

15

"It does not. The tech to destroy ourselves already exists and we don't have the wisdom to control it."

"Humans often do act like the silly primates they are," he observed gravely. "So how do you plan to spend the end of days?"

"I'm visiting friends in Chicago before heading home. Beyond that, no immediate plans. You?"

He held up his paperback and shrugged. "I don't think humanity has near as much time left as you do, actually. I've got a good book. I predict it's going to spread like a fire across the world and take much of humanity with it."

I chuckled though I noticed the hawk-faced man did not. "Oh? There are a lot of books out there. What makes this one so special?"

"That's the mystery of it, the code beneath a code that unlocks the end of the world as you know it."

"Like a puzzle book? Or a choose-your-own adventure?"

"You could say that but maybe more like a book of wishes and curses. I'll show you." He held out the book and fanned the pages, flipping leaves too quickly for me to scan the book's contents. "Stop at any page."

I had the distinct feeling he was about to perform a magic trick. His offer sounded too much like, "Pick a card, any card!" Without thought, I reached into the flipping pages to stop them. A shiver jangled up my arm as if I'd plunged my hand into a pool of glacial water.

The stranger opened the book for me and gestured for me to read the passage I'd randomly chosen. It was an odd list of nine words arranged in three groups in no order that had meaning for me:

Hampstead, iron, enemy.

Chalice, gates, opprobrium.

Steel, uroborous, sonder.

"IT'S GIBBERISH," I said.

"Read each group of three as if they were one word. Try it aloud. Shove the pieces together. That's how you make magic words and words magic."

"Hampsteadironenemy, chalicegatesopprobium, steeluroborous-sonder." I made a face. "Still gibberish."

He turned the book toward himself and read, "And with these three keys, the secrets of the universe could be unlocked, buried again or destroyed." He closed the book with a thump, apparently pleased with himself. "Good for you! You have begun!"

"Achievement unlocked?" I asked.

"Out of context, I am sure it makes no sense to you. That's because it's all so new. Don't worry. All will become clear."

"What's the magic trick, though? What was that supposed to do?"

"It's what it doesn't do to you. In reading all three codes and *not* being affected, you've passed the obstacle that will open all the other possibilities to come."

It was about that moment I wished I'd continued to pretend to be asleep. My mother warned me never to speak to strangers.

4

THE KEY TO A LOCK

The hawk-faced man had a cruel slash for a mouth which did not improve his looks when he smiled. He had long teeth and more, it seemed, than are usually allotted to a human being. "Books can be an excellent escape and a defense against strangers, don't you think? A day without reading is a day that is not done. Shall we try my trick with your book and see what we find? May I see yours for a moment?"

I shrugged my agreement and handed over the paperback. He was careful to maintain my bookmark, a simple slip of paper. Rather than read the description on the back of the book, he closed his eyes as he flipped pages. Seemingly at random, the stranger cut in with a flat hand. His fingernails were long and dirty. I thought of talons.

My traveling companion opened his eyes and read, "All language began as magic spells. You see? The universe is winking at you. The extraordinary is often disguised in the familiar, hiding in plain sight."

When I failed to react, he asked me if I thought it was true that language may have begun as magic spells.

"Fanciful," I said without commitment.

"But true, I think. Prayers are magic words. People give them weight, do they not?"

"I've never known a prayer to be answered."

"Perhaps you were praying for the wrong things."

"By my lights, that's far too convenient."

He seemed unperturbed by my skepticism. It was easy to imagine him as an avuncular professor who was far too full of himself. I suspected we had a little in common that way. I knew a lot of obscure things no one cared about, too.

"Language is a code we learn to decipher," he said. "All of life is constructed from an alphabet of DNA. A, T, C, G. That's only four letters."

"It's not four letters," I objected. "Those letters represent four nitrogen bases — "

"Adenine, guanine, thymine and cytosine," he said, "The little acorns from which great oaks grow. My point is that based on very little, we have all life. From simplicity we get infinite complexity given enough time. Do you enjoy music?"

I admitted I did, of course. His question sounded odd and too generic. People generally asked if you like opera or country or rock and roll. Music is far too broad a term.

"I love music," he said. "I love it because it is a universal language. It is the chaos of noise brought to order. Have you considered that a little strip of magnetized tape can contain the complexities of every recorded symphony? Imagine what still may lie undiscovered in the depths of the unconscious amid the skeins of neurons and the explosions of electrochemical signals bouncing around the insides of human skulls."

I glanced down at my book. "I've read something that hinted at that idea recently."

"Synchronicity! That's the universe winking at you, again, letting you know you need to sit up and pay attention."

"I don't know — "

The hawk-faced man plunged on, pressing home his point as if it were the sharp end of a spear. He nodded at the book in his hand, turning it over and over as if it gave him an unfamiliar tactile pleasure. "People deal in words but never consider their deeper import and potential. Music is a language but words in the right order are a kind of music, too, don't you agree?"

"I never really thought about it."

"Most haven't, but there is a sweet vulnerability in a book. In the space of a few words, the author's mind meets the reader's mind across time."

I felt like my seatmate was carrying the bulk of the conversation so I offered, "I think I know what you mean. I reread *War of the Worlds* recently. There's a moment when the alien emerges from the spaceship that really creeped me out. Pretty impressive considering the forces combatting the aliens arrived with horses and wagons."

"Excellent. Words touch the heart, they seal lifelong vows — "

"Start wars — "

"And end them," he interjected.

Feeling a little fatigued, I nodded genially and wondered if I could get back to sleep.

The stranger tipped his head closer and asked, as if sharing a secret, "You understand how a novel can transport us elsewhere, maybe place us together on a train bound for Chicago, for instance?"

"Huh?"

"You haven't considered the hidden code within the code. A particular arrangement of words can unlock something, something hidden within the consciousness that is waiting to be released."

"Uh, like what? Are you talking about those strings of words strung together? Didn't work on me."

"But in others, the right words in the right order might harness the killing power of guilt. Guilt and regret can be so strong that such emotions can release the human death drive. You really don't believe in the power of words?"

Stepping into General Pitmore's presence could easily and instantly give me a stress headache. Emotional upheaval can yield physical pain. It can even deliver a mortal punch. Broken Heart Syndrome, where a recently widowed spouse dies soon after a beloved partner, is a real thing. So were the many instances of

PTSD leading to suicide. "Saying the wrong thing at the wrong time could set off a biological response that ends in tragedy, sure," I admitted.

"Sabina Spielrein originally proposed the phenomenon of the death drive. Freud stole it years later. Have you ever felt the pull of the space in front of an oncoming subway train? Surely, you have. That brief impulse is the death drive."

"Sounds like the opposite of the survival instinct. I'd venture the will to live is a lot stronger in people."

"Perhaps but that inkling to stop the struggle is instructive, is it not? What if that specific impulse could be triggered and amplified?"

An involuntary laugh bubbled out of my throat. I didn't mean to make fun of this strange man but it sounded like he was proposing that people had a self-destruct device embedded in their DNA.

"Taken as a collective," he continued smoothly, "I'd suggest the death drive is strong in the human race."

"Nah, that's probably just our short-term thinking and unwillingness to delay gratification at work. If the death drive were strong, we wouldn't have survived this long."

"Ah, but now you have the tools to commit mass suicide."

Was that a hint? I wondered if he knew what I really did for a living.

The hawk-faced man steered away from the topic of weapons of mass destruction, however. Instead, he used the example of climate change. "The aversion to dealing with that existential threat could be an example of the death drive at work, could it not? Many will deny climate change until they're drowning. The death drive is always bubbling beneath the surface. It's more common than you think."

"Suicide is usually mental illness or just being too damn old or sick and tired of suffering, isn't it? I'm a bit tired and I have a headache. I'm sorry I've lost the thread — "

"Words can do lots of things … soothe, inspire or distract." He shot me a toothy grin. "What if a book could trigger it? Surely you believe in the power of words to change the world?"

"If the orator is great, maybe. I don't think a book can be weaponized — "

He scoffed, suddenly impatient. "Of course you do! Why have propaganda departments, otherwise? Why kill all the intellectuals and enemy writers at the beginning of every revolution?"

Ready for the conversation to be over, I conceded, "I take your point."

"When you think about it," the stranger continued, "we're all using our words to pray constantly. Lovers whispering words of love are praying to be loved in return. A child's cry is a prayer for comfort, food and care. Every single utterance is a — "

"I'm an atheist," I replied flatly.

"Then when you speak, you're praying you're right about everything. The religious and the non-religious share a common trait. They're both hoping to make sense of the world and each side assumes there is sense to be made."

"I doubt that commonality will bring us together."

"You're probably right. The only thing that seems to bring people together is a common enemy. Humans are such a violent species."

"You talk like you aren't one of us."

He gave me that toothy grin again and another cold shiver crawled up my spine. "We aren't one of you but for the sake of world peace you will be one of us. You are the messenger, Lieutenant Colonel."

I had given him my name but I hadn't said anything about my rank. "Who are you and what do you really do?" I demanded.

"My identity is of little consequence. After this meeting, you will not see me again. What matters is what you do next. You are in a unique position to help us. With this book, you could save many lives."

5

THE SPYDER'S WEB

The stranger flipped to a page near the front of the book and showed me the text.

And God said,
"Let there be Right!"
And there was Right.
He saw that it was good.
On the sixth day,
He introduced the variable
that would doom the project.

HE SMILED WIDER and I saw even more teeth, long and thin and packed tight. "It would seem God has a gift for curses. This book will bring about the fall of everything you know. After that will come a new era and, with your help, it could be a utopia."

"Utopia literally means 'nowhere.' It's a fantasy built out of air. I deal in math about the end of the world. I know the variables. There are always too many permutations. I think one of us had better move to another seat on this train. The strain of thinking about the end of the world is why I'm on this vacation."

I looked away, embarrassed. I had stopped short of confessing to a crazy stranger that I was on medical leave. To my relief, my seat-mate did not pursue my unguarded remark.

"There are so many variables," he agreed. "This book is the new variable in your calculations."

"You seem to know what I do for a living so let me tell you this: Conspiracy theorists show up at Cheyenne Mountain quite frequently. They all demand to be let in so they can see the aliens they think we've got locked up there. I don't have time for their nonsense or yours."

By his placid expression, I could tell I had no effect on his mood. "From my observations from on high, there are certainly such things as curses. You're about to find that out."

"That sounds like a threat."

"No. I am here to prepare you. I will leave you in a moment, I promise."

He reached out and put one cold hand on my arm. I stiffened at first and then found myself relaxing, mesmerized by all those teeth. The train car seemed to melt away and I felt like I was in a sound-proof room in a cloud of cotton.

I stared openly at my seatmate's mouth and, for no reason I could understand, sank deep into my seat. Tension drained from my muscles. It was as if I was alone with the hawk-faced man, not just one-on-one on the train but alone in the black sea of a starless sky. I couldn't hear the noise of the California Zephyr burning through the night. I couldn't hear anything except the stranger, my breathing and my heartbeat. The pace of my heart slowed and my body seemed loose at the joints and longer.

When I spoke again, I was surprised to discover the anger had drained from my voice, too. Now I was merely curious. "I haven't felt like this since I had too much tequila the day I graduated from Officer Training School at Maxwell. What is the point of all this?"

"Just as I said: preparation," he replied. "You strike at my wonderment, Zane. You are an atheist mathematician and yet I am sure you appreciate nuance. I must ask you to consider my question seriously: Do you believe in curses?"

Reluctantly, I gave a small nod. "I only know of one, maybe, just because it's so damn weird."

"Tell me."

"After this, you will leave me alone?"

"Absolutely. Your free will is very important to me. Come what may, the choice must be made by a human."

"You're weird," I said.

"I'm sure I must seem that way to you."

It was rare for me to talk to strangers, much less talk about such questions. "My father is a pharmacist but he's also a gearhead," I began. "He loves cars, especially old American muscle cars. He likes the growl of those big engines. We went to car shows once in a while."

"And that was his curse? Not being able to possess what he desired?"

"No, no. Let me finish so this can be over. I'm talking about the James Dean car. When I was a kid, Dad told me about it. My father made me wonder if a curse could be real. The story goes that as soon as the actor Alec Guiness laid eyes on James Dean's Porsche 550 Spyder, he told Dean it would kill him. Seven days later, Dean was killed driving that car. The weirdness only begins there. That car, even parts that were sold off from that car … they killed, injured and maimed many people. It fell off a transport trailer several times and crushed the driver of the truck. When thieves went after it, even they were injured. It's just the strangest damn story ever. No one knows where that car is now."

"So maybe a cursed object is a thing?"

"Not really but — "

"But?"

"I'll only say that the story is so weird and the calamities were so relentless, it gave me pause."

The stranger nodded and let go of my arm. I fell out of the

black sea. I could hear the percussive rhythm of the train on the track again. As my senses began to return, my heart began to race again and I wondered if it would burst out of my chest.

6

THREE KINDS OF PEOPLE

"There are three kinds of people, Zane," the stranger told me.

I quirked an eyebrow. "Only three?"

"We are all made to fit in God's hand. We are each either a Tool, a Weapon or an Instrument."

"If you're right, my guess is we're toys in the claws of a monster."

"Toys? That would fall under the category of Instrument."

"Oh."

"I wish I were like you, Zane. Loss Prevention, indeed! Too many euphemisms: Homeland Security, Department of Defense."

Before I could object or pull my arm back, his long-fingered hand clamped on my arm again and I found I could not speak. The stranger leaned back and indicated a passenger across the aisle I had not noticed. He was a large fellow so I couldn't imagine how I missed him, especially since he was quietly weeping.

"I read a few pages to that gentle soul. The poor fool assumed he was an instrument. That's not fair, really. He was an instrument of a sort."

Blinking hard, I found that I could still breathe but I could not breathe a word.

"Sadly for him," my seatmate continued, "he doesn't believe in what he did for a living anymore. We had quite a chat while you were sleeping, he and I. He used to call himself a healer. Through the power of love, care, placebo and neuroplasticity, he did some people some good. After our chat, he realized what he'd done for most of his life makes him a fraud. There are many kinds of Instruments. He falls into the subcategory of Pawn. He was much happier when he believed his bullshit. His sin is Pride and, as we all know, that precedes a fall."

My jaw worked but no sound came and I could feel the prick of tears in my eyes.

"I think of myself as one of God's Tools but the book can be a Weapon. Just like you, Messenger." He opened his mouth wide as his face split into a grin and I thought of feral, starving animals eager for the kill, desperate for a bloody feast.

The train car swayed and clacked along but the lights dimmed. "You'll have to excuse me. It's been lovely speaking with you. I have to go have a chat with the conductor now. He thinks his wife is faithful to him during his many absences. It's time to harness the power of disillusion. Humans are so in love with their illusions of high ideals that when the truth hits, they all fall a long way down."

He dropped my book back in my lap and got up to leave. The last thing I remember before I lost consciousness was the hawk-faced man standing over me and whispering softly, "Everything that is about to happen is predestined. It's a script you cannot help but follow but the final choice must be yours. The fate of humanity must lie with a human and you, Lieutenant Colonel, have been chosen to carry that great moral burden. I apologize. You did not ask for this, but it is necessary."

I fell into darkness that yielded to a long, oddly familiar nightmare. I tried to escape but I felt like I was trying to run through thick mud. It was up to my waist and tried to suck me under. When I say *tried*, I mean that literally. The mud had a force of will and its intent was to drag me under and fill my lungs. I struggled but lost ground.

Worse, someone was watching and unwilling to help.

Worse than that, I could feel the weight of Doom's cold shadow. Something unnamed and unknown was bearing down on me. It might have been a large predatory bird. It might have been a man with wings and talons for hands.

I awoke at dawn as the California Zephyr pulled into the terminal in Chicago. The book I'd brought with me was still in my lap. The large man who had sat across the aisle was already up and joining the line to the exit door. The hawk-faced man was nowhere in sight.

When I was a small child, I thought a fitful sleep meant a satisfying and deep sleep. A few years later, I learned it meant a sleep "full of fits." I guessed I'd fallen into a dream woven into a nightmare. I had been under a lot of stress lately. Stress plus an overstimulated brain made some sense of my encounter with the strange stranger.

The illusion held for a moment. I could have dismissed it all and tried to forget the vivid dream except for the stranger's book. It lay in the seat beside me.

I put my book into the bag between my feet. I could have left the book of curses behind but I was too curious for that. After only a moment's hesitation, I picked up the abandoned paperback.

It was fairly slim. The cover featured an enigmatic figure standing under a clock in a field of fire. I probably would have passed it over had I spotted it in a bookstore. However, the tome felt heavy in my hands, heavy with mystery and a need I could not identify. Its cover was surprisingly cold to the touch just as the stranger's touch had been.

It was not curiosity alone that made me take the book with me. I was overcome with the odd feeling it was not only *meant* for me, but that it was *waiting* for me.

When I looked up from my seat, I glimpsed the large man who had sat across the aisle as he disappeared from view. I had questions and he could be leaving with the answers I sought. I needed to talk to that man, to find out what he knew.

Hurrying to catch up, I took the curse with me.

7

DUSK AT DAWN

I t is an odd feeling when you are sure you are being watched. Of course, I had no evidence. No one hid among the seats and as I peered into the next car, I saw passengers lining up to exit the train. I yanked my bag down the aisle to disembark and hurried after the large man with whom the stranger had spoken.

I was the last to leave my car and, as I stepped down from the train, a crowd of other passengers streamed past. Chicago's Union Station is the fourth-busiest terminal in the United States. I should have gotten up and pursued my quarry as soon as I'd come to. I had not imagined that such a large man could melt into a mass of travelers so quickly. It was as if the throng had purposely swallowed him.

Women wearing bonnets and long black dresses passed me carrying very young girls in similar dresses. The group was followed by a stout man wearing suspenders and a straw hat. Mennonites of some traditional stripe, I caught snatches of German as the man spoke to the women in stern tones. On their heels came a couple of very earnest-looking young men wearing white shirts, dark ties and black pants.

I extended the handle on my bag and its wheels whirred behind me as I raced through the swarm of humanity, dodging left and right. The crowd was too thick and the exits too few for me to run in a straight line for long. Despite Union Station's size, the sheer numbers of people clogging the building's arteries made their pace positively viscous.

Impatient to find the large man, I was sure I could spot him if I could gain enough ground and find a choke point where he was likely to pass. I was paying more attention to the flow of the crowd than I was to where I was going and got lost for a couple of precious minutes.

Who was the hawk-faced man? Had he poisoned me somehow? Was it exhaustion? Was I sick or cursed from reading his magic words? Was I being watched and if so, by whom?

Maybe this is some new kind of bizarre test, Zane. If it is, you're failing.

Forget curses and nightmares. The most likely scenario was that someone from my government or a foreign power was screwing with me, trying to compromise me in some way. Was it the FBI? Was I under investigation? People with my level of security clearance had to expect scrutiny. Despite my years of service, there was always suspicion, always the possibility of being compromised. It wasn't necessary to do anything wrong to lose security clearance. Having a secret anyone could use against me would be enough. A year ago I'd been interviewed about the student debt I still owed.

My suspicions were ramped up because the previous week I'd had an awkward discussion in a staff meeting and my superiors didn't approve of my opinion even though they'd asked for it. I should have read the signs before Lieutenant Havelston warned of my jeopardy. Pitmore was trying to get me to back off from my complaints about the pace of replacing outdated equipment. Though his reasoning was flawed, people on my team got quiet whenever I entered a room after that.

It was possible Pitmore could have put in a call to someone to see how I reacted under stress. Even as I considered the possibility, it sounded too elaborate and paranoid.

Maybe, Zane, old buddy, old pal, the problem is that there really was no hawk-faced man at all. Check your bag again. Are you even sure the book is still there? Maybe you're off your nut.

As soon as I decided I had failed to find the passenger from the train, I rushed to the passenger concourse. There the crowd thinned somewhat. Fewer exits led from the train platforms. Scanning the crowd and panting hard, I came up empty. I paused to study the signs for Riverside Plaza, the bridges and Madison Street. At a whim, I headed for the largest exit onto Canal Street.

Early morning sunshine bathed me in orange light as I stepped onto the sidewalk outside the station. People hustled back and forth. I studied the crowd. There seemed to be more cigarette smokers here than in Colorado. I was sure I'd lost the other passenger who had spoken to the stranger.

Or maybe he's a figment of your imagination, too, Zane.

That voice in my head was my own and the doubt in my sanity was growing fast. My doubt would soon be big enough to carry me to a mental health institution and out of a job. "I'm not crazy," I said aloud.

If you're wondering if you're crazy, don't ask a crazy person, came the quick reply.

Then I spotted the large man from the train. He stood at the edge of the street between two food trucks. I shouted, "Sir! Stop!"

Passersby looked up but did not move. They followed my gaze as I ran toward him. It seemed as if everyone was watching now.

"Sir! You in the plaid shirt! Hold up a minute!"

The man glanced down at his shirt, turned briefly and looked back toward me. Pain etched his face. His eyes were wet.

"I need to speak with you," I said. "There was a man on the train — "

"The bird man," he said.

Taken off guard, I paused, unsure how to proceed.

"He showed me his book."

"Me, too," I replied. "He did something … I'm not sure but it was like he knocked me out. I don't know how."

"I wish he'd knocked me out."

The man was somewhere between thirty-five and forty-five. He had a moon face, jowly and soft. His was one of those faces in which you can see the child he'd once been. He looked as confused as a lost boy.

"You never met him before?" I asked.

"He sat beside me on the train. I was asleep and when I woke up he was beside me. I don't know why he chose me. Why the hell did he have to choose me?"

"He told me he was some kind of accountant."

"I got the feeling that was some kind of inside joke."

"What was his name, sir?"

By his blank look, I could tell he was searching for an answer. He'd come up empty just as I had.

"What did he tell you?" I pressed.

The man took a deep breath but shuddered as he exhaled. Damming up his emotions, I sensed his control was fragile. On the edge of a crying fit, he said, "He showed me the way things really are, the meaning of things. There's a lot less meaning than I thought there was. He got inside my head — "

"Mine, too. I just don't know how."

"He didn't tell you?"

I suspected I knew the answer but was too embarrassed to say so.

"He did tell you, didn't he?" the man asked. "You just don't believe him." He studied my face. "You don't *want* to believe."

"He talked about curses and secret codes."

"Do you know how this ends?" the man asked.

"How what ends?"

He looked around and smiled for the first time. He gestured to the city around us and shaded his eyes against the rising sun. "This. Everything."

Before I could tell him I didn't know what he was talking about, he uttered one last word.

"*Chalicegatesopprobrium.*"

"What?" It was one of the phrases I'd read aloud for the stranger.

"I'm not sure it has a direct translation into English but I have a sense of its meaning."

"Yes?"

"Carrion comfort from the necessary dead."

The necessary dead. I knew that phrase well. It was a term we used at Cheyenne "for tactical projections of the number and scale of death caused to innocent civilians by kinetic action." Collateral damage was the common term. On the graveyard shift, when fewer staff were around, the gallows humor came out. Then we called the necessary dead something grimmer: human sacrifices.

The man screwed up his mouth, trying to formulate a more coherent response. "You know how they say, 'The truth will set you free?' Whoever is in charge left out something important. Before you can go out that gate, the truth has to shatter everything first. It'll break your bones and drain you of blood. We have to feed Death. We're what it needs. We're the necessary dead. To get where we're all going, we have to pay."

"Pay who?"

"Cover me in ketchup," he said. "I'm ready."

He leaped into traffic. Though the driver of the UPS truck stood on his brakes, the man went under the screeching wheels and flopped dead before the truck could skid to a bloody stop.

8

THE ROAD LESS TRAVELED

I stood frozen for a moment. The man's head was squashed flat. A woman in a big sun hat grabbed me by the shoulder. "What did you say to him?"

Dazed, I stared at her in numb horror. "W-what?"

"I saw you talking to him. Why did he do it?" Her voice climbed higher. "What did you do, mister?"

A guy standing in line at the food truck looked angry but not so concerned he was prepared to give up his space in line. He glared at me. "Did the guy get pushed? Did that guy push that guy?"

He was pointing at me now, ready to throw around accusations but God forbid he miss out on his bagel.

God, I thought, *people are such assholes.*

I ignored my accuser and stared helplessly at the carnage beneath the UPS truck. I didn't want to look but found I could not look away or even move. I'd seen bodies in caskets at funerals. I saw my grandfather in a hospital bed just before he died amid a plethora of useless tubes. Medicines and saline solution flowed in as hope and bodily fluids drained. The tubing looked like the same stuff I'd used in my fish tank as a kid.

My grandmother on my father's side died of a heart attack in her garden when I was away at college. Nothing in the military or out had prepared me to witness a person taking his own life in such an abrupt and horrific way in downtown Chicago at the beginning of what should have been a beautiful sunny day.

In shock and wordless, I just looked back at the woman in the floppy sun hat. She kept talking at me, a torrent of words, but I wasn't processing anything. In my eyes, her face transformed as she spoke. She changed from a middle-aged white woman into an angry, shrieking chimpanzee. She clutched at my shoulder and said something about calling the police.

I shrugged her off. My head throbbed and my stomach turned. I leaned against a wall and bent from the waist. My guts lurched. I was ready to vomit but nothing came. I had not eaten since the day before. I had nothing to give up to nausea.

Two strong hands gripped my shoulders and someone called my name. It was as if the voice was reaching me from a long distance, echoing down a tunnel. I straightened, expecting to find the angry chimp woman in my face once more. Instead, I found my friend from college, Aleksander Nowak. Alek was supposed to be my ride from Union Station and I was very glad to see him.

"Zane? You okay?"

I pointed toward the street. "I saw it happen right in front of me. I'm okay, I just didn't expect it."

"Understandable." Whenever he concentrated or was worried, his forehead formed a dozen deep horizontal lines. He always joked that he had an old man's face and that one day he would grow into it. Despite his typically stoic tone, his forehead was creased like a very old man.

I first met Alek in university. He had more hair and a whip-smart girlfriend named Charlotte then. The hair deserted Alek but Charlotte stayed on to become his wife. I couldn't wait to get back to the safety of their home.

"How'd you find me?" I asked.

"I didn't really. I was waiting for your text when I heard the screaming." Alek gestured vaguely toward the cluster of onlookers gathering around the UPS truck.

Some milled in circles, shaking their heads. Others stood still as if they'd been arranged in a horrific tableau. Someone was *still* screaming. I guessed it was the Chimp Woman. I may have gone into shock briefly but she probably started the day unhinged and things had gotten worse from there.

"You saw the accident. We'll have to wait for the police. They'll want a statement."

"I was just talking to the guy just before he went under the wheels. I did not see that coming."

"Who was he?"

"A passenger on my train. I don't know his name. We didn't sit together. I don't even remember where he boarded. That poor driver didn't have a chance to avoid him."

"You sure you're okay? When I looked back and spotted you, I thought maybe the truck had clipped you, too. You look very pale, Zane."

"I'll be fine. Shock."

"I would have thought you'd seen the same or worse in your business."

"A drone strike from 30,000 feet is quite a bit different," I said.

"Well, not to sound like an asshole or anything but welcome back to Chicago," Alek replied grimly. "What do you say we get out of here?"

"But I should speak with the police. You said so."

"I just thought better of it. There are plenty of witnesses. Let's just get out of here."

I looked around and heat rushed to my scalp. "My bag. My bag is gone! I had a small black roller suitcase. I must have … I had it with me when that guy killed himself. I must have left it by the street."

We hurried back and searched between and under the food trucks. My eyes darted to people in the crowd but no one held my case.

Alek told me what I already knew and did not want to acknowledge, "Sorry, it's gone, Zane. Stolen."

I cursed long and hard, blowing off tension. The lost clothes could be replaced but I'd shoved my phone in the side pocket along with my money and ID. That would be a huge hassle. "Now I have two things to speak to the police about."

Alek dug out his phone. "I'll take you out to lunch later. We were going to order in tonight and Charlotte's making sweet potato pie. I'll text her to let her know we'll be late but we'll get this sorted out. You'll need to cancel your credit cards and so forth. I'll skimp on the details. I don't want to upset Charlotte. She's about to burst."

Charlotte was pregnant and due soon. It was their first child and I was to be the child's godfather. Coming to Chicago for a vacation from Cheyenne seemed the most logical thing. I could see my godchild before abandoning my friends to the joys of parental bliss. At that moment, I wished I'd settled for pictures on Facebook. I could have been on my way to the Dominican Republic or Costa Rica but instead, I'd chosen a train ride to Chicago. That choice had earned me a weird conversation with a very strange man followed by a lot of trouble.

"I'm glad you're here," Alek said. "Char needs cheering up. She's very sick of being preggers. If the baby doesn't finally come this week we're going to induce next Tuesday. You get to help me put the crib together, buddy."

"You haven't done that yet?"

"You sound like Char. She got me to paint the nursery in the first trimester. I've been dragging my feet on the other preparations."

"Why?"

"If I build the crib, it's all real. I'm not ready to be a dad, but ready or not they'll go in after the little critter next week. Guess I better get my head around it, huh?"

"Better warm up those cold feet. It's too late for that. You guys put off having a kid forever already."

"Almost too long, Char says."

"Grow up and get excited about the baby," I advised. I couldn't understand how he could feel otherwise.

Alek said more but I was distracted. The screams were still going on and the mayhem wasn't coming from the suicide scene. All heads turned to look at the woman in the sun hat.

She stood on the sidewalk, her head tipped back so far that her hat fell off. She wasn't saying words, or at least not English words. Her screams formed a jumble of vowels and sharp consonants.

I turned to Alek, thinking he might translate. "Is that Polish? Do you understand what she's saying?"

"Nah, that's not Polish, you clod. I don't know. Could be Gaelic. Sounds like gibberish to me."

"Chimp Woman," I said. "I can't tell if she's howling in pain or just really pissed off."

9

FATE IS A WAVE

Several onlookers were on their phones, calling the authorities. Only a couple of minutes had passed since my fellow passenger had jumped into traffic but it felt like much longer.

Alek stared at me quizzically. "The guy who killed himself must have triggered her into psychosis."

Triggered into psychosis, I thought. *That puts a more rational face on the hawk-faced man's talk of curses.*

"What did he say before he threw himself under that truck?" Alek asked.

Feeling helpless, I shook my head. It was too much to explain. "Now I have three things to talk about to the police."

"The suicide and your stolen suitcase," Alek said. "What else?"

"It's complicated. I think a man I met on the train slipped me some acid or something."

Before Alek could respond, Chimp Woman screamed louder, mostly vowel sounds now. She began to tear her hair out. Tufts of blonde and gray hair came away in her fists. Her scalp bled and red rivulets ran down her face but she kept going.

A man and woman rushed to her side to stop and soothe her. She pushed the Good Samaritans away with surprising strength.

The man was shoved back several paces and the woman fell to the sidewalk. The back of her head struck the sidewalk with a sickening wet smack and then more people started yelling. Some started up their cell phone cameras while others screamed for police.

The first responders had already been on their way. A police cruiser pulled up beside the UPS truck. More sirens wailed in the distance as two officers — male and female — emerged from Union Station's Canal Street entrance.

As the cop in the car jumped out he was drawn to the sidewalk by all the screaming. He paused only a moment to assess the situation. As he strode past me, the officer reached for the radio mic at his shoulder and called for an ambulance.

The police who'd been on patrol in the train station reached Chimp Woman first. I stared at her face. It was no longer the visage of an angry chimpanzee. That delusion had passed but her screams did mimic an ape's angry shrieks.

The couple who had first rushed to stop Chimp Woman were at her feet and no longer paid her any attention. The man knelt over his companion, gingerly holding her head wound. A pool of blood spread out beneath the stricken woman but she was still conscious. She was crying and repeated only one word over and over: *Why?*

"Jesus," Alek said. "The world's been going crazy for a while but it feels like the decay is speeding up all of a sudden, doesn't it?"

Though Chimp Woman was older and quite slight, the pair of cops went after her as if it was a football tackle in a grudge match. Her sandals flew off as she went down. Though she went down hard, she kept screaming. Squirming onto her back, she managed to kick the female officer in the face. We all heard her bare heel strike with a surprising ringing sound. The officer's head rocked back and when she brought her chin back down, Chimp Woman nailed her in the face again, digging in her heel, flattening the cop's nose.

Bystanders winced at the sight. Some shook their heads in disgust and dismay. I noticed that a few who were recording the melee, presumably for distribution on their social media accounts, laughed. Seeing their casual disregard for others, I felt a twinge in my stomach again. "People really can be such incredible assholes, Alek."

Two young men who stood near Alek and me wore identical t-shirts sporting the emblem of the Illinois Institute of Technology. They stared, their jaws slack with surprise.

"Can you believe this shit?" one said to the other. "Did you see that? That old white lady is fighting the cops like they're babies! Like babies!"

"That's hardcore MMA for you," his friend replied. "Every-body's getting into it. Don't mess."

As the cop from the police cruiser got to the struggle on the side-walk, he reached for his handcuffs. "Pin her! Pin her, for God's sake! Get her on her stomach!"

Chimp Woman surprised us all again. As the male officer strug-gled to flip her over, she reached for his holster. As she pawed at it furiously, the cop yelled for her to stop. She managed to yank the weapon out anyway.

"Gun! Gun!" the cop from the police cruiser yelled. He dove for the weapon as the crowd scattered. Two muffled pops in quick succession.

The screaming stopped and there was a moment of silence as fresh shock set in. The cop who had momentarily lost control of his weapon was holding his pistol again. He let out a torrent of angry curses. The female cop ignored her smashed face and rolled the woman onto her stomach to handcuff her.

The cop who had arrived in a cruiser sat on the sidewalk and barked into his radio. "GSW! GSW! Where's that ambulance?" He glanced over his shoulder at the woman whose head had struck the sidewalk. "Two casualties." Then he glanced into the ruined face of his fellow officer and added, "Make that three and a dead one under a truck. I need a supervisor out here immediately."

"Alek," I whispered.

My friend seemed to come out of a trance. "Huh?"

I pointed. Beyond the dying Chimp Woman, I spotted my suit-case. It lay on its side. The book lay splayed on the sidewalk beside it.

I willed my legs to work again and Alek trailed behind me. The scene seemed to shift into slow motion as I passed. The man who'd been part of the Good Samaritan couple still cradled his partner's head. The woman's eyes were glassy. I guessed that if she wasn't dead already, she would be soon.

The cops seemed to each be in their own worlds. The one on the radio was still talking. The female cop was holding her broken nose, waiting for the bleeding to stop. The third cop sat on his haunches, his pistol still in his hand but apparently forgotten.

I heard their prisoner, too. Bleeding from the abdomen and gasping, she was saying something that came like a stage whisper, delivered with a seductive cadence that made me slow my pace.

"Fate is a wave that crashes upon us," she said. "We swim against the current, tire and succumb. This is the way of all things. Despite my best efforts, like you, I am just another thing among many. But know this, as it says in the *Bhagavad Gita*, 'No one who does good work will ever come to a bad end, either here or in the world to come.' This is my fate and I'm getting what I deserve." Alek placed a hand between my shoulder blades and urged me forward, gentle but firm. I nodded and moved but I was still a bit dazed. Three dead on a sunny July morning under a sunny Chicago sky. There was no need of it but I was beginning to suspect the true cause.

I strode to my suitcase and righted it. My money, ID and phone were still in the side pocket where I'd left them. The book I'd bought in Colorado was in the case with my clothes, too.

Scooping up the book the hawk-faced man had left for me, I glanced down and spotted the first sentence: *Fate is a wave that crashes upon us....*

"Fate," I muttered to myself. "Fuck Fate."

"Seneca said Fate leads the willing and drags along the unwilling," Alek said. He reached out to take the book from my hands but I slammed the book closed and stuffed it in the case before he could see the words.

"What the hell is going on, Zane?"

"Hell is here. We need to get away."

PART II

Doom rushes upon my enemies.
To each his own death
according to his deservedness.

I imagine one of the reasons people cling to their hates so stubbornly is because they sense, once the hate is gone, they will be forced to deal with their pain. ~ James Baldwin, *The Fire Next Time*

DESPERATE AND DANGEROUS MEN

Alek and Charlotte lived in Bridgeport. As Alek drove, he rehashed what we'd seen. Flummoxed by the sudden violence, my friend went over the scene, again and again, trying to make sense of it.

"That was the *damnedest* thing," Alek said in a mystified tone.

Damndest, I thought. *Or damned.*

I mostly stayed silent. I worried that whatever details I could share would sound too crazy. The stranger on the train had said something about all of creation being just fine until people were added to the mix. It seemed to me that spilling my guts to Alek about everything would add to our confusion rather than adding clarity.

Traffic wasn't bad so we pulled into Alek and Charlotte's driveway within forty-five minutes. Before we got out of the car, Alek stopped me. "Hey, Charlotte's super pregnant, so take it easy on the details, please. She's more sensitive lately."

"*Our* Charlotte is acting sensitive? She swears like a sailor and is addicted to true crime podcasts."

I was working on my master's degree when I met Alek and Charlotte. After attending a lecture on game theory, I wandered into the University of Chicago Pub. The couple who would become two of my best friends were at the next table arguing about the lecture I'd just attended.

Alek was a fan, soft-spoken and enthused about the possible business applications of the science.

Charlotte would have none of it and didn't hold back. "Game theory assumes everyone is a rational actor. What evidence do you have of that? That's not merely stupid, it's obviously counterfactual. Don't be stupid!"

I burst out laughing and, since I was alone, it was clear to them that I'd been eavesdropping. Charlotte thought I was laughing at her and was not amused. "Do you have something to share with the rest of the class?"

"Sorry," I told them. "I was just at that lecture. You have a point. According to game theory, the buildup of nuclear weapons is a sound strategy."

"How do you figure that?" Alek asked.

"Because my master's thesis is on the flaws in strategic nuclear defense planning."

"So you're saying you agree with me?" Charlotte inquired.

"Absolutely!" I hefted my glass of beer in a toast. "Respect!"

"Hey, Duke Nukem!" Charlotte replied. "In that case, join us and the conversation."

It was hard to picture Charlotte becoming squeamish. Alek nicknamed her Charlotte the Bold after she asked him on their first date. She spotted him across a cafeteria and asked him out immediately. It was she who asked him to marry her, too. He'd been reluctant and she often joked about dragging Alek down the aisle against his will. Char had never been a wallflower.

"My sainted wife has been quieter since she got into the third trimester," Alek told me. "She's worried about the world we're bringing our kid into."

"All parents everywhere have worried about that forever, except maybe in Switzerland and Costa Rica. From what I hear, those countries have their happiness on target lock."

Alek allowed a small smile. "Maybe don't mention the flattened head under the truck, okay? You turned green when you saw it and Charlotte had a rough first trimester. Lots of throwing up. We got through that without her killing me. I don't want an encore."

I agreed. I didn't want to dwell on that image, either. I also knew I'd carry that memory for the rest of my life.

As soon as we came through the front door, Charlotte called from the kitchen, "*Halloo!* Alek, is that you?"

"Burglars!" I called back. "Two of us, desperate and dangerous!"

"Fine! The silverware is in the hutch. I never use that fancy shit, anyway. There's a little cash in the junk drawer in the kitchen but if you come after my sweet potato pie, I will cut your throats!"

I gave Alek a look. "Sounds like the same old Char."

"The old Charlotte would have said she'd gut you and strangle you with the entrails."

"Oh, that's right. She's from Maine."

We chuckled at the old inside joke. Alek's parents were very conservative Polish immigrants who had settled in Wisconsin. Charlotte was from Bangor. They say opposites attract and I took Alek and Charlotte as prime examples of that adage. Shy and quiet, Alec had planned to manage hedge funds but didn't like the people or the pace.

Confident, exuberant and relaxed, Charlotte convinced her husband to switched career tracks and open his own small financial planning firm. Alek's parents hated her for it.

I never figured out what their problem was with Charlotte. She could be coarse around the edges but she had a good heart and a good job. She was on leave from an information management job at Chase Bank.

"I'm fat!" she called out again. "I can't waddle out to you so come to me! I'll give you a hello hug."

I did as I was told and walked into the kitchen. "Is there pie? I was told there'd be pie."

Charlotte rushed to me as soon as I entered the kitchen and hugged me tightly. "Zany! It's been too long! Facebook updates and

Twitter and the odd phone call doesn't cut it! How many years has it been?"

"A few years and about nine months, I'd say." I pulled back to look at her belly. It was evident she was incredibly close to giving birth. "You aren't fat. You're full of baby."

"I look like an apple, a pregnant apple. I can't wait to get back to Pilates and squash but right now I'm having a hard time with shoes. Even my feet got fat."

"You look beautiful, as always, Char."

"It's the damn hormones. They give my cheeks color. I can't wait to get back to looking pale and anemic. Are you gonna stick around for the birth? Alek will need help with all the poopy diapers. I'm going to need to be treated like a queen for a while, say the next eighteen years until the kid goes off to med school."

"I'm just in town for a few nights. I don't want to get in the way of you guys bonding with Baby Nowak."

"I'd ask how they're treating you but I know any tough questions like 'how are you' are deep threats to national security and the safety of the free world."

"I'm … okay."

I thought I'd sold the lie but Alek did not have my poker face. Charlotte's face fell as soon as she turned to look at her husband. "What's wrong?"

Before I could think of something vague to say, Alek crowed, "Blood, bullshit and weirdness!"

"Well, hell, do tell!" Charlotte said. "Sounds like Zany's come to Chicago and brought demons with him."

11

SINGSONG WARNINGS

Now that I'd entered the hearth and haven of their home, I didn't want to shatter the peace. I wanted a warm kitchen filled with the smell of a baking pastry. Sweet potato pie and domestic bliss sounded wonderful. It felt like something close to the ideal norm.

"There was some awful trouble downtown," Alek began for me.

"You don't want to hear the details," I said.

"What kind of trouble exactly?"

"A suicide, assault and a homicide!" Alek said. "They happened within a few minutes of each other and what? Maybe a hundred feet, Zane?"

I tried to shrug it off but Charlotte was too quick. "*That* can't be a coinky-dink! Where did this happen?"

"Canal Street, outside Union," Alek said. "We saw it all up close. Zane was right next to the suicide guy."

I shot my friend a dark look. "Alek, I thought you didn't want to get into the grisly details."

"There are grisly details? Well, now I have to hear them."

"Charlotte," Alek said. "What about the baby — "

"New strategy, dear husband and gent. The baby doesn't speak

English yet. It's true that God made us sensitive, irrational, and relatively hairless anxiety monkeys so let's not feed into that more than we have to. It's bad for the little critter's development. We don't have to cover the kid's ears, though. Just speak in gentle singsongy tones so the baby's subconscious isn't wounded. Children with PTSD from bad childhoods become financial planners."

Charlotte winked at her husband at that crack and Alek held up one pinky finger.

"Wrong finger!" I said. It was another old joke among us but it had staying power.

At that moment all three of our phones blared like sirens. Though it was unfamiliar to my friends, I recognized that unique sound right away and the danger it could signify. One of my duties was to represent the Air Force with the group that implemented and maintained NCSS, the National Civilian Signaling System. "It's a Homeland Security alert," I said.

"What's that about?" Charlotte said. "Am I going to have to put on a sweater and fill a bag with cans of beans or something? Fill a bathtub full of water for drinking?"

"The mission of the United States Air Force," I recited, "is to fly, fight and win in the air, space and cyberspace. That noise you hear is freedom calling."

"Does freedom have to be so goddamn loud?" Charlotte complained. "It's so jarring — "

"They don't want you to relax and ignore it," I said. Choosing the sound of the alert had been the subject of two research studies. Determining how many decibels the alarm should be had taken up almost two months of committee meetings.

Charlotte touched her belly and paused before she was ready to check her phone. She sang softly in a sweet voice that took on the tone of a child's lullaby. "This fucking kid is killing me with all the kicking. I think she's wearing cleats. If she grows up to be a soccer player, Alek's dad might finally show me some fucking respect."

"But probably not," Alek warned.

My phone was still in my bag, vibrating and ringing much

louder than I preferred. Homeland alerts override any setting on any phone.

Alek turned the screen of his phone toward me. "Looks like you lucked out, Zane. You missed a train derailment."

Charlotte read her phone, as well. "*Two* trains. They're saying it's a terrorist attack."

"Where?" I asked.

"An eastbound and a westbound train. Head-on tragedy. It just happened. How could they know it's terrorists so quickly?"

I shrugged. "The NSA might have heard cyber-whispers of an attack for months but didn't have enough specific details to stop it or issue a warning before the tangos hit."

Charlotte returned to her singsong tones for the baby's sake. "I'll tell you one thing. Between the stuff you saw downtown and this? It's all a bit too train intensive and train adjacent, isn't it? You guys are going to end up talking to the FBI before this is over. It's all connected. Trains are safer than air travel — "

"Maybe air travel got to be too hard a target," Alek suggested.

"The Transportation Security Admin. does have those roving VIPR teams," I said.

Charlotte quirked an eyebrow at me. "Homeland employs killer snakes?"

"VIPR: Visible Intermodal Prevention and Response."

"They worked really hard to come up with a cool acronym that only sort of fits, didn't they?" Charlotte observed.

"They didn't do anyone much good this morning," Alek said sourly. "Death and destruction. This is terrible!"

"Guys!" Char reminded us. "*Gentle* indoor voices, remember?"

"Or maybe we could each just have an internal monologue and keep our darker thoughts to ourselves," Alek suggested meekly.

I had assumed Charlotte was only half-serious but she kept it up as she sang gently, "That's downtown. See something, say something, sure, but as my dad used to say, we're safe as houses. It's scary and horrible but you know how terrorists are. They're one-pump chumps. Now that they've shot their wad, it's over. I doubt Death has come to Bridgeport." She shot us a reassuring smile.

"You're going to be a great mom, Char," I said.

"Fucking right I am! I'm going to miss the cusses, though. I figure I can let loose as soon as she hits school age. Little kids swear up a storm, anyway. Princess Nowak will have to be prepared for the real world. They don't tell you that in the child development books but I remember. I went to school — "

"Yeah, but that *was* Bangor — "

"Shut up, Zany."

"You got it, Char."

I studied Alek's phone. Details were sketchy and since the media reports were all fresh they would undoubtedly be wrong. Early bulletins screw up the body count and even the revised estimates of casualties could not be trusted until they were made official. That could take days.

Then I remembered the last words the hawk-faced man said to me. He'd said something about how he had to go speak with the conductor. A cold shiver jangled up my spine.

The fear must have registered on my face. Char noticed it first. "What's up?"

"This is going to sound crazy," I said, "but I think there is the equivalent of a nuclear weapon in Bridgeport." I looked askance at my suitcase.

Charlotte's confident smile faded. "Oh, my nerves! You ain't shittin' me in my own home, are you, Zany? That would be rude."

"It's a fairly theoretical concept in weapons research but, uh … wow."

"Yes? Wow what?"

"Wow and woe. It's going to be hard to explain but I think there might be such a thing as a mind virus. I've seen it at work and, if I'm not entirely crazy, I think I've got the trigger in my suitcase."

12

THE MIND VIRUS

"If you're not entirely crazy." Alek crossed his arms and gave me a look I recognized from old arguments. He didn't believe me. "If you're thinking this is hypnotism, it's not. You can't get people to murder anyone or kill themselves. Stare at a watch and give them suggestions all you want, they won't do it unless they wanted to do it anyway."

Charlotte was at least willing to listen. "Are you talking about those CIA Manchurian candidate experiments? Like with LSD?"

"Project MKUltra, you mean? Maybe something like that. The CIA says all those brainwashing experiments are off. Sometimes I wonder if someone somewhere at Homeland is still toying with menticide experiments. The Department of Homeland Security is an umbrella for at least twenty-two agencies. There's gotta be at least a few blackened bananas in that bunch."

"Hold up. Menticide? That's a new one on me," Alek said.

"Wipe out the normal cognitive functions of an individual and reprogram them to your own script. That's menticide. I'm not sure about the mechanism."

"But you think the man on the train drugged you," Alek said.

"Sure seemed that way. I don't know how. Transdermal patch or

… poisoned pages in the book, maybe? All I remember is having a weird conversation with him and then I passed out. I woke up in Chicago and people started dying. I remember he touched my arm. I held his book and maybe on the pages — "

"What book are you talking about?" Charlotte searched our faces.

The truth sounded too ludicrous. I considered holding back but Charlotte and Alek were my best friends. "My hypothesis is that there's a book in my suitcase that kills people with words, triggers them somehow — "

"Yeah, right." Alek didn't care to conceal his disdain. "Between this train tragedy and the things we saw this morning, I think you're letting your imagination get away from you."

I'm sure he meant well but his doubting interrogation irritated me. "Did you not hear the woman the cops shot?"

Alek shook his head. "She was babbling and muttering. I didn't catch anything much that made sense. This was the one … what did you call the woman the cops shot?"

"Chimp Woman."

"Right. Wasn't she the one who you said harassed you in the street? She wasn't stable to begin with, Zane. You know that."

"Alek!" Charlotte said sharply. "Ease off. Don't make me yank your leash. You know where the leash attaches when they lead monkeys around, right?" Apparently, Charlotte had given up on the calming and cooing approach to protecting her fetus from angry tones.

"Okay, okay," I said. "I know how this sounds but I'm telling you, I heard the woman on the ground quoting a passage from the book. The man on the train left the book for me and it's like an infection. Chimp Woman and the suicidal guy … why would I lie, Alek?"

He shifted back and forth on the balls of his feet. "I'm not saying you're lying. I'm saying you're mistaken. There has to be a logical explanation. Have you ever checked out how illusions are achieved? Look up magic tricks on YouTube. The trick to how the illusion is achieved is always disappointingly simple. You said you've been under a lot of stress lately. What about mass hysteria? Like what happened with the American diplomats who thought they were attacked by a sound weapon in Cuba? That wasn't exactly a hoax but they were mistaken."

"First off, I'm not so sure that wasn't a legitimate attack."

"Oh, c'mon!"

"Second, mass psychogenic illness made a bunch of people in the Middle Ages dance until they dropped. We still don't understand the dancing plague very well — "

"I know this feels intentional to you," Alek said, "but the evidence is circumstantial and the effect is not mass anything. The train accident — "

"It's not an accident. It's a terrorist attack."

"It's a warning of a terrorist attack. They couldn't know for sure this quickly, surely?"

"Threat assessment is part of my job, Alek."

"Maybe the job has made you too paranoid and too quick to pull the trigger."

I hated my friend's oh-so-reasonable tone.

"Alek. *Sh.*" Charlotte gave me another hug and patted me on the back. "I believe you. Alek will, too. Just tell us more."

"The guy on the train said he was going to go talk to a conductor — "

Alek interrupted me again and this time he made an incisive point. "If the book triggers suicidal or homicidal intentions, how come you aren't dead? You read from it, right? And he didn't actually *give* you the book, did he? The man on the train left it behind. If you wanted to spread mayhem and destruction, would you leave it to chance and just leave it lying around for a stranger to pick up or pass on?"

Charlotte came to my defense again. "Who wouldn't have picked up the book, though? It was a virtual certainty. Curiosity killed the feline."

"And maybe three people on Canal Street," I added.

"We're getting a little too much exercise jumping to conclusions," Alek said. "Chicago has a pretty high murder rate — "

"I'm telling you, Alek! It's me! Can't you see — "

"You haven't answered my question," Alek pressed. "If your suspicions are true, why aren't you dead or pulling your hair out?"

I took a deep breath. "When you don't know the answer to a question, the right answer is, 'I don't know.' I don't know. All I do know is, the guy on the train told me I was a weapon. He said I was 'the messenger.'"

Alek harumphed.

"You know I hate it when you harrumph, Alek."

"How many times have you told me Zane means 'gift from God' and Salvador means 'savior?'"

"Maybe a dozen and always as a joke."

Alek shook his head. "I think you're taking yourself way too seriously, man. Sorry, but c'mon."

"'C'mon?' I guess I can't argue with that depth of logic."

I wasn't sure how much Charlotte believed but she was a better listener. She was also practical. "Let's suppose for a moment that every bit of this is true. Is there anyone on Earth you can call who won't immediately put you on a seventy-two hour psychiatric hold?"

I had serious doubts a call out of the blue to the authorities would be fruitful. I couldn't even convince one of my oldest friends who had witnessed the incident on Canal Street. "I know someone I could call," I said. "The trouble is, I'm not in the best position for a fair hearing with my superiors right now."

The doorbell rang and Alek looked down the hallway. "Who is it?"

Someone pounded on the front door. "FBI! Open up!"

I didn't get a chance to go to the authorities. Somehow, they'd found me.

13

ONE KIND OF POSSESSION

"Sounds like come what may is here. I better go deal with come what may." I told my friends to stay in the kitchen. I paused just long enough to grab my military ID card out of my bag before heading to the door. A male voice called my name and pounded on the door the whole time I walked up the hallway.

A young man and a middle-aged woman waited on the front stoop. I had the guy pegged right away by his aggressive look. He stood straight and stiff, a six-foot tall hard-on hiding behind aviator glasses. I could tell the female agent was more experienced and relaxed by the way she slouched.

When I thought of the FBI, I usually pictured a crew in dark suits who all seemed to have the same tailor as the President's Secret Service detail. It was either that or FBI black and yellow wind-breakers over bulletproof vests. This pair broke the cliche. The man wore a loose-fitting jacket and gray slacks with what was, I assumed, a coffee stain. The female agent wore jeans and a brown leather jacket. They stared at me as if they'd already asked a question and I had refused to answer.

"Can I see some ID, please?" I asked.

The woman showed me her FBI badge. "Agent Bonham," she said. "This is Agent Askey."

The man just stared at me. Apparently, he thought I should be satisfied that one of them supplied some evidence of authority. I guessed that was good enough, too. The fact that they knew who I was and where to find me was pretty good evidence they were exactly who they said they were. Federal agents are pretty good at tracking phones.

"Let's see your ID." Askey held out his palm.

I held up my military card for them to see but I didn't hand it over to him. "Is this about this morning on Canal Street?" I didn't want to end up in a psychiatric hospital so I took Charlotte's hint and shut up about the book.

Askey gave me a look of feigned surprise. "Why would you ask that? We didn't say anything about Canal Street."

"Yeah, you got me, Sherlock. The only other thing anybody could complain about is an outstanding parking ticket. I haven't got around to mailing in the fine. Is the Federal Bureau of Investigation tracing people for outstanding parking violations now?"

To my relief, Bonham took the lead. "You left the scene of a murder. We have you on camera — "

"Conduct unbecoming, isn't it?" Askey broke in. He spoke like an angry prosecutor, as if I was the accused sitting on the stand.

"I imagine you have a lot of people on camera, including having the whole thing recorded. If that's the case, I can't imagine why you'd need me."

This seemed to deflate him a little so the woman took up the torch with which they planned to burn me. "There was a terrorist attack this morning, Mr. Salvador."

"I just heard. You guys are fast."

Bonham squinted a little. I knew that trick. When you keep half a squint, you blink less. The result was she looked watchful and not a little like a robot. "You were inside Union Station this morning?"

"Along with hundreds of others, sure. Thousands, probably, huh? Chicago's always a hoppin' town. It must be all the tourists coming to be disappointed by the pizza that's really tomato, cheese and bread cake."

"Where were you inside the terminal?"

"I came from Colorado Springs. I don't know what platform but I left as soon as I could. It was a very long trip and I was anxious to get out."

"You stood out on the surveillance cameras," Agent Bonham said. "You were running through the station."

"Really? The only one? I was in a rush to catch a ride from my friend. But you got me. It's true, I didn't stop at the Cinnabon."

"People are dead. You're pretty damn flippant about it and wasting our time," Askey said.

"I'm not the one wasting time. You're asking questions you already have the answers to. I know you have a job to do but I don't see the point of this interview. Is this the part where I ask if I'm being detained? Should I call my attorney? I don't actually have one but my friends probably know a few."

Bonham looked at her partner for a long beat and pointed with her chin toward a black SUV double-parked in the street. The agent glowered at me before turning on his heel to return to his vehicle.

I called after him, "You dress like shit, Askey! Have some pride and buy a decent suit."

He scowled back at me as he got into his car.

"Does your partner understand that 'if looks could kill' is just an expression, Agent Bonham? Anyway, now that you've gotten rid of Junior — "

"Shut it. We both know looks don't kill. Words might, though."

I took a long breath to slow my thudding heartbeat. *I'm not alone in this, after all,* I thought. "You're looking for the book and the hawk-faced man?"

Bonham brightened a little. "Hawk-faced man? *Heh.* I hadn't thought of him that way but that sort of fits."

"I only met him last night and — "

She held up her palm as if it was a stop sign. "You've got the book?"

"Yes."

"Good. We worried you'd lost it in all the hubbub."

"I've got it. Do you want it?"

"Hell, no," Agent Bonham said. "I don't want anywhere near it. We just needed to make sure you still had it in your possession."

"I don't understand."

"You'll receive instructions when the time comes. That'll be soon. You have no idea the depth of the shit you've stepped into. Not yet. You will get it, though. In case you haven't figured it out already, you're being monitored. I can't stress enough how important it is that you hold on to the book and do as you're asked. For everyone's sake, do as you are asked."

I stepped back inside the doorway. I wanted the option of slamming the door in the agent's face. I had so many questions. I didn't get a chance to ask one.

Behind me, I heard Charlotte scream. It could only be Charlotte. It wasn't the sort of squeezed-out shout that made me think she'd gone into labor. It was the sound of a person in fear for her life.

I turned to rush back down the hall and looked back for a second, gesturing for Agent Bonham to follow me. She did not follow me. She was hurrying back toward her car.

Askey revved the engine and barely gave his partner time to jump into the passenger seat before roaring off down the street.

Charlotte screamed again. "Zane! Help!"

14

ANOTHER KIND OF POSSESSION

When I got to the kitchen door, I found Alek and Charlotte standing on opposite sides of their round kitchen table. He wore rubber gloves meant for washing dishes. In his right hand, he held a cleaver. My roller suitcase was tipped over at his feet and the stranger's book lay splayed on the floor.

Before I could speak, Alek leaned forward to swing the cleaver in a flat arc, vicious and lethal. The blade missed his pregnant wife's throat by inches. Charlotte kept the table between them but the kitchen was small. She would not be able to shuffle out of the way for long.

"Alek!" I yelled. "What are you doing? Stop!"

His forehead was shiny with sweat. Deaf to reason, Alek didn't even glance my way and he did not pause. Not content to chase Charlotte around the table, he hauled back and threw the cleaver with all his might.

By sheer luck, the blade missed Charlotte's head. The cleaver hit a cabinet full of dishes which rattled and shook from the force of his throw. The tip of the rectangular blade almost stuck in the wood but the heavy handle drooped and the cleaver clattered to the floor beside Charlotte.

"Jesus, Alek! You've got to stop! Stop! Stop! *Please,* stop!"

Alek ignored her and strode to the knife block on the counter. As he withdrew a long blade, I grabbed a heavy wooden kitchen chair. My intent was to keep him at bay long enough for Charlotte to escape. I held the chair with the feet pointing toward my old friend as if I was a lion tamer who suddenly found himself without a whip and without a gun. "Hey! Hey, Alek! Look at me!"

His single-mindedness worked to my favor. Alek was so intent on murdering his wife that he did not spare me a glance as I ran at him with the chair. As he crashed into the counter, I yelled for Charlotte to run.

I managed to delay him but he was neither injured nor discouraged. Alek struggled briefly. I could not pin him for long. He had always been naturally thin so, with a twist of his torso, he slipped between the legs of the chair. The knife was pinned to his side but not for long and we were suddenly inches apart.

His breath hit my face as he grunted and wrenched the knife free. The blade was meant for carving turkey. He held it in his fist in an overhand grip. He held it high in the air ready to plunge the dagger down into my face, my neck and my organs.

I pushed off from the chair and dropped it as I wheeled backward and tripped over my suitcase.

On the floor at his feet, I was at his mercy but I could only detect murderous rage in his face. My calm, rational friend whom I'd known for over a decade was gone. He was fury incarnate and focused on me. Alek took a step forward, towering over me as I began to scramble to my feet.

I knew I would not be able to get out of the way fast enough and held my arms up to try to ward him off. The words *defensive wounds* came to me then. Surely I would fail and Alek would stab me with the long blade, again and again and again.

At that moment, Charlotte saved me. She leaned out from under the kitchen table and drew the edge of the cleaver's blade through her husband's left Achilles tendon. The sharp blade slid true and clean. Alek howled as he went down on one knee. Blood spray hit the kitchen cabinets and began to pool around him.

Charlotte tried hacking at his hamstrings but that attempt was not nearly as successful. The cleaver ripped through his pants but he shifted away so he caught the flat of the blade. It wasn't much more than a stainless steel spanking.

Alek growled like a feral animal and turned to bare his teeth at his wife. Charlotte had incapacitated her husband somewhat but Alek still held the blade in his fist.

But she bought me time.

I was on my feet again and he was teed up for a field goal attempt. When I kicked him, the toe of my shoe caught him in the softness of his throat and his head snapped back. The knife dropped from his hand and he crashed back into the kitchen cabinet. Weakly, he tried to get up but the floor was becoming slick with his blood and he slipped back down, choking, gasping and coughing.

With tears streaming down her cheeks, Charlotte crawled out from under the kitchen table. When I helped her to her feet she still gripped the cleaver. I doubted she would let go of it so I didn't even try to take it from her. I stooped to snatch up the long blade Alek dropped.

Charlotte edged around her fallen husband. She put down her weapon but only long enough to grab the big wooden knife block. She unceremoniously chucked it out of her kitchen window over the sink. In one fell swoop she succeeded in shattering the glass and got the most obvious weapons out of the room.

"Good call," I said. "Thank you."

"Thanks? Don't be stupid. *Jesus! Call 911!*"

"Right. Have you got something to tie him up with?" I asked.

"Never mind that. Call 911. He's hobbled. We've got the knives. Even in my condition, I can outrun him, or at least waddle at high speed. Don't go near him. He's … uh, Alek might be infected or something."

She looked down at her hands. They were covered in blood. She ordered me to watch her husband as she returned to the sink to run hot water and dish detergent over her hands.

It finally occurred to me why Alek had worn the rubber gloves. He doubted my speculation that the book's pages were covered in some kind of mind altering hallucinogen. He'd taken the precaution just in case my guess was right. My guess was wrong and it had nearly cost Charlotte and the baby their lives.

Charlotte leaned heavily against the sink. She was due soon and I worried this trauma would crank up that process.

Alek's chest muscles appeared to be in spasm as he struggled to pull breath past his broken throat. I worried that I'd done permanent damage. He didn't seem to be able to get enough air in. Each breath came and went in a wet wheeze. I'd never kicked anyone in the throat before.

My hands shook as I dug out my phone. "What the hell happened in here? I was only gone for a couple of minutes!"

Charlotte's gaze fell on the book. "Curiosity killed the feline."

Of course, it did, I thought. *What was Charlotte's phrasing? Who wouldn't have picked up the book, though? It was a virtual certainty.*

Alek had always been an intellectually curious fellow. He'd been skeptical of my claims but he had to know for sure. I had an uncharitable thought then: What had been more important to my old friend? Had he wanted to prove me wrong or to prove himself right? Perhaps he'd taken Charlotte's credulity as a subtle insult. Had it been pride that caused him to defy my warning of the book's danger? Was it some kind of competitive instinct, trying to prove to his wife that he was the rational one?

In her left hand, she held the bloody blade, ready to deal a death stroke if necessary. Her right hand cradled her swollen belly. For a moment, the kitchen was filled with the sound of Alek's tortured gasps and Charlotte's sobs. I had brought misery to my friends and I hated myself for it.

"911, what is your emergency?" The dispatcher's voice was calm and flat.

My voice shook as hard as my hands as I stammered that I needed an ambulance.

"The address is … " I blanked and looked to Charlotte. I could find Alek and Charlotte's house in the dark after a long night of drinking but I didn't know the house number.

"We have the address," the dispatcher said.

"You better get the cops here, too," I said. "My friend went crazy and attacked us. He's had a … a …."

"What has he had?"

"Uh, a psychotic episode, a violent psychotic episode. His name is Aleksander Nowak. He attacked his wife and me. She's pregnant, very pregnant. She'll need to get checked out, too. We've managed to subdue him but — "

"What is his condition now?"

"Bleeding."

"Is he incapacitated?"

"Yeah, for now. Are they coming?"

"You need to get out of the house," the dispatcher said, "and be sure to take the book with you."

"Wh-what?"

"I'll send the ambulance and take care of Charlotte," The dispatcher said it in that same flat tone. It was as if she was dictating the details of a recipe. "You need to leave, Zane. Any attempt to destroy the book will result in Charlotte and her baby's untimely death. Do you understand? You better. Get out of there now. If you are on the premises when the ambulance arrives, Alek and Char-lotte and the girl who was to be your godchild will die. Go now. Tell Charlotte you were never there and she's never heard of the book."

"I don't understand."

"You don't have to understand. You have to do. But it is your choice. I'm just telling you the stakes."

I didn't hesitate. "Okay."

"You will receive further instructions. We're sending you your very own guardian angel." The line went dead.

My voice sounded hollow and I felt empty as I stared at my friends spattered in blood. "I'm sorry, Char."

To protect Charlotte and the baby, I had to do as I was told. There wasn't really a choice. My course was set, a virtual certainty.

15

JAMAICA

First, the FBI had turned its back on trouble. Now an emergency dispatcher was part of this strange conspiracy. I reasoned that it probably wasn't a Chicago EMS dispatcher I was speaking to. More likely, it was the FBI rerouting the call from my cell phone to mimic the real thing for their own purposes. But what were those purposes?

"Come," I told Charlotte. "He could still be dangerous to you. They're coming. Leave Alek. Come outside to wait for the ambulance."

I grabbed my wallet and phone. Last, and careful not to look at the text, I grabbed the book from the floor.

"Leave it," she told me. "Or burn it."

"Can't." I shoved the book under my shirt and under the belt at the small of my back. "I can't leave it behind."

"Why the hell not?"

"Because it's a weapon. Because they know that I'm supposed to be your child's godfather."

"Who does? I don't — "

"The dispatcher! I don't have time to explain even if I knew what to say. I have to leave. When you talk to the cops just say Alek had a psychotic break. Don't even tell them I was here. If you do, I think you're in danger."

We left Alek alive and coughing in a pool of blood. "They'll get here in time to stop the bleeding," I assured her. "He'll need a transfusion — "

I should have left right away but as we made it to the front step Charlotte leaned on me so hard I worried she would fall. I encouraged her to try to take slower, deeper breaths. Once we were out in the fresh air, Charlotte leaned against the stair railing and gulped in breaths as if she were drinking water. In tears, she asked what would happen to her husband.

"I don't understand this but once the doctors get hold of him, I'm sure we'll get some answers." I wasn't sure but it was the thing to say.

"You're going, Zane? Where?"

"I don't know yet. Someone's supposed to show up to tell me what's next. I will find a way to contact you and when I do, we'll both know more. I'm so sorry this happened. I don't understand it."

She nodded but I saw anger in the set of her jaw. Anger often comes on the heels of fear.

In the distance, I heard sirens. Her knees were still shaky so I offered her a hand and helped lower her to the step.

"Your bag! Go back for your bag!"

"Right!"

I took one of the steps before reeling back. Alek stood in the doorway. He'd left a trail of blood as he limped out of the front hall's gloom. The walls to the narrow hall were covered in streaks of blood and bloody handprints. With great effort, he'd come close to sneaking up on us. He held a shard of glass from the broken kitchen window in one hand.

"Stop right there," I told him. "The ambulance and the police are coming."

Something about him had changed. He wasn't an animal on a rampage anymore. Perhaps it was the blood loss or the kick to the throat but he didn't look aggressive anymore, merely lost. He looked back down the hallway for a moment and his gaze paused at a picture of him and Charlotte that hung on the wall beside him.

"Jamaica." His voice cracked and I guessed his windpipe was swelling with inflammation as he croaked, "It's all my fault."

Charlotte didn't seem to have the energy to get up. She stayed seated but turned her body. "Alek? What is it? Why?"

"Jamaica is where it started. I didn't know it at the time, but that was our last free moment ... at least until the credit card bills started coming."

"Where what started, love?" Charlotte probed gently.

"We couldn't really afford to go," he said weakly. "We can't afford this house, this kid...."

Tears streamed down his face as he looked at the shard of glass in his hand. Its sharp edges had cut his palm. He was bleeding there, too.

I stood between them. I couldn't simply leave him alone with Charlotte. "Please put that down, Alek. It's hurting you."

My friend looked at me sharply. "I resented you, Zane. Free as a bird, living in the mountains. I've always wanted to live in the mountains or by a beach. You complain about your job but your responsibilities are so ... theoretical. You're off doing your job and you think the world's at stake but the planet just keeps on spinning. *Hmph.*" He winced. "I am not good at my job. I lost a lot of money. I spent a lot of money. It wasn't all my money, either."

"What are you saying, Alek?" Charlotte asked.

"I cooked some books, played around with the spreadsheets. I started taking some. It was just enough skim off the top to help with the mortgage at first. Last week, I used embezzled money to buy the fanciest bassinet and the most expensive baby carriage I could find. I'm sorry, Charlotte. I wanted you to think ... I wanted you to respect me."

"I do, love. I do!" Fresh tears streamed down Charlotte's face. "Why? Why didn't you tell me — "

"I expected more of myself," Alek said. "Good schools, good job ... I messed up somewhere along the way. I took a wrong turn and missed the train. We are all pretenders. We pretend it will all work out okay. We act like a good end, the happy ending we expect, is guaranteed. Everything is so much more tenuous than that. I thought I was a good person. I used to think I was special. We are all so damn entitled."

"It's going to be okay, Alek," I said. "We'll get you some help — "

"The worst part is, later, after Jamaica, I started to see how entitled you were, Charlotte. I started to resent you and the baby. I spent more money than I have. I spent on myself, too, *just* for myself. I started to hate you almost as much as I hate me."

"Alek! Stop!" I implored him. "You're not yourself. None of that matters," I said. "Not compared to — "

"Of course it matters!" Alek's voice was suddenly stronger and he spoke with the passion only the crazed and people of utter conviction can muster. "It matters to me and it matters to the book! And this is me. In this moment, right now, I'm more myself than ever. See me!"

Alek stabbed himself in the throat with the shard of glass as an ambulance pulled up to the curb with its lights flashing. He did a thorough job of it, slashing himself from ear to ear. My friend fell forward and collapsed on the front step face first. He'd lost a lot of blood but he had more to give. Blood gushed from his carotids and jugulars. In the time it took for the EMTs to get out of their rig and grab their gear, he was already a dead man.

I retreated down the steps to avoid standing in a pool of blood. I stared at him, baffled. I'd known Alek for a long time. I rarely made it back to Chicago but we spoke on the phone often. If anyone had asked if Alek was capable of doing anything criminal, I would have laughed in their face. No clues, no hint of resentment had ever passed his lips in all the time I'd known him. To all appearances, he was content and successful.

It crushed me that in the span of a few words squeezed out of his swelling voice box, I believed him. Alek's confession, I was sure, was not the result of an induced psychosis. He hadn't been honest with me or with his wife before but his dying actions betrayed the underlying truth of his words.

Charlotte, still seated on the top step, turned her back on Alek. His blood soaked her maternity dress but she did not move. Instead, she covered her eyes with her hands, pressing the palms to her face.

"Charlotte?"

Just above a whisper, she said, "Go. Just go."

The paramedics did not spare me a glance. They rushed to Alek first but abandoned him to his fate as soon as they turned him over. Then they began to assess Charlotte, asking about her wounds to determine how much of all this blood was her own.

I left my bag behind and slipped away. Whoever was running this conspiracy would have to forgive me for not going back for a change of clothes.

As I turned away, I heard Charlotte say, "Well, isn't this a colossal confluence of fuck?"

16

A GATE AND A PASSAGE

I strode down the street, away from prying eyes. More sirens sounded nearby. They were coming, whoever *they* were. Maybe the pair of federal agents I'd met on Alek and Charlotte's stoop would return to make sure I'd followed orders. They couldn't have gone far.

I worried Askey and Bonham might kill Charlotte if they spotted me anywhere near the place. As I passed a lamppost I smashed my phone against it and discarded what remained of the device in a garbage can by a bus shelter.

With that baffling crime scene only a couple of blocks behind me, a young Asian woman in a classic powder-blue Stingray cut me off at the crosswalk. Through the open window, she called my name.

"Who the hell are you?" I asked.

"I'm the one giving you a ride."

"Maybe you're not. Seems a lot of people aren't what they say they are all of a sudden."

She fixed unnaturally bright green eyes on me and I froze. I was so rattled I almost complimented her on her contact lenses.

"I don't like it any more than you do," she said. "Get in the car. They may be watching."

"Who is *they?*"

"If you don't get in this car, I'm supposed to take the book and find someone else. You don't know it yet, but you don't want that."

"Don't I?" I wondered if I could unload the responsibility of carrying the book.

"It's up to you," she said.

"What is this, exactly?"

"You ask more questions than I anticipated."

"So answer one."

"You're in the saving the world business, are you not?"

"Ostensibly."

"This is that. The trouble is, you're the best candidate. Decide quickly, please. Time is short."

Motorists began to line up behind the mystery woman's car. They honked their horns angrily and their urgency cut my deliberations short. Figuring I could learn something from this mysterious stranger, I hurried to hop into the seat beside her. "Got a name?"

"I am Quire."

"Miss? Missus? Doctor? Madame? Mister? Is that a first or last name? Code name?"

"Just Quire."

"Great. Where are we going?"

"To begin, those in charge want a famous person. You're about to meet Lil' Pomp, formerly of the band, Lil' Pomp and the Circumstances."

"The rapper?"

"His star is on the rise. He just changed his name again. He calls himself Rhythm Method now."

"Clever."

"Is it?" The way she said it sounded like a genuine question.

I shrugged. "It's not like I know him. Why would this guy talk to me?"

"The book will take care of that."

Two police cruisers and another ambulance shot past us, sirens blaring. "Can you tell me if Charlotte is okay? I got out of there as quick as I could — "

"Not my department." She sped up and pointed the Stingray's nose toward Streeterville.

I had more questions. Quire ignored me and didn't speak again until we arrived in front of a large house surrounded by an iron fence. At first, I thought it was a huge duplex but it turned out to be one large residence. Behind the iron gate, a large muscular black man sat in a lounge chair smoking a blunt.

"Get out of the car," Quire instructed. "I'd suggest you take the book with you."

"I don't understand what you want from me."

"Perhaps if you show the man at the gate the book you will gain more clarity of thought and intention. Allow him to choose a passage. As soon as he finds the words, he will be in that passage."

"In it? I don't get the metaphor."

"You don't have to understand it. Experiment. After you gain more experience, you'll have better questions and you will be able to accept my answers."

I thought of Charlotte, pregnant and inconsolable with her husband dead on their front step. I had brought this tragedy to my friends' door. With Charlotte's fate at stake, I didn't know how to stop and get off this horrible ride. For my friend and her baby, I did as ordered. I told myself I'd stop the spread of the mind virus at my first opportunity. How much damage would I be blackmailed into doing before I found a way out?

I waved to the man behind the gate. "Hi!"

He looked me up and down, seemed to decide I was harmless, and gave me a small smile. "Hey." He took a long drag on the blunt and, after holding the smoke in his lungs, slowly blew rings.

Quire stood behind me. The man behind the gate took longer looking her up and down. "Hey." He favored her with a bigger smile.

Quire nudged me forward.

"We need to see Rhythm Method," I said.

75

He didn't move from his chair. "Y'all don't have an appointment with Mr. Method. Nobody does. He's busy. Sorry, folks."

I began to turn back but Quire grasped my elbow and stopped my retreat cold. "I've come a long way for this."

"Y'all need to move on down the sidewalk now. It's a beautiful day and there's a lot of sidewalk. You should go explore. See the Bean. Shop the Miracle Mile with the other tourists. Eat up at the Cheesecake Factory. I recommend the Blue Man Group. Anywhere but here, okay?"

As I pulled the book out of the back of my pants, the guard shot out of his chair and pulled a pistol out of his waistband. As soon as he saw the book in my hand, he giggled and the tension went out of his body. "Man, you came so close to getting yourself plugged, I can't even tell you. A split second the other way, you'd be split down the middle and shitting yourself blue."

"Sorry. I ... uh ... have you ever seen this book?"

He glanced at the cover. "Nah, man, nah. Remember what I said about sidewalks? Mr. Method is not seeing any fans today. You want to see him, you gotta buy a ticket to a concert like everybody else, please and thank you."

I looked to Quire, expecting her to interject. She glared back at me but remained silent. When I turned back to the guard, his gaze was fixed on the book.

"Hey, now ... what is that about, anyway?"

I didn't know what to say. "I met a man on a train who said it had a code hidden in it."

"You mean like a puzzle?"

"I guess. I don't understand — "

"Hand it here a sec."

I offered the paperback through the iron bars and he flipped through it. "No puzzle here."

Quire nudged me and I blurted, "Pick any page."

He shrugged and stopped somewhere late in the book. He paused on a passage and muttered aloud, *"Parabellumotisaccura."*

"Does that mean anything to you?" I asked.

The guard handed the book back to me. To my great relief, he placed his pistol on the seat of the lounge chair carefully. So far, the only effects I'd witnessed were extremely negative: suicide or homicide or both.

"I've taken a wrong turn," he said. He opened the gate, swung it wide open and pushed past us. "I gotta go back."

"Where?" I asked.

The guard did not answer and my escort hushed me. "That's his passage."

She pulled me through the open gate as the man strode down the sidewalk. He moved like a man who was very late for an important appointment. Quire took the pistol from the seat of the chair and dropped it in her purse.

"He isn't going to do something he shouldn't, is he?"

She shot me a look that was hard to interpret. I wondered if she felt a little sorry for me. "Doing something he shouldn't is not what epiphanies are about."

17

UNDER A GIANT HAND

B efore I could question her further, Quire ushered me to the front door. I was about to ring the bell but she stopped me, took my hand, and placed it on the door handle. I obliged and pressed the button, swung the door open and stepped into a stranger's home unannounced.

A speaker hidden somewhere in the ceiling announced in a soothing female voice, "The front door is ajar."

The house was large, bright and clean. It looked like a model home prepped for sale, as if the rooms were for show, not for living in. There were no pictures or personal possessions in evidence. It didn't look like anyone really lived there except for the scratches in the dark hardwood floor. I peered closer at the damage and thought, *Skateboard*.

A moment later I heard footsteps coming our way. I wanted to leave but Quire seemed placid, as if nothing that could happen would ever surprise her.

A man's voice echoed down the hall. "Durrell? That you?"

Before anyone could come around the corner and catch us unawares, I called out, "He left!"

"Left? Durrell left? What do you mean he left? Who's that?"

"That's him," Quire told me.

A skinny, shirtless young man covered in tattoos came around a corner. I hadn't expected him to be Caucasian. The last white rapper I knew on sight and could name was Eminem. After a moment, though, I realized I did, in fact, recognize the musician's face. I wouldn't have been able to name him but I knew him from somewhere. I had never paid attention to the red carpet before award shows. I wasn't sure how I knew his face. Perhaps I'd seen his picture on the front of a tabloid or part of a meme on social media.

The internet was a carrier of its own kind of mind virus. Unbidden thoughts and images could find anyone with a phone and an idle moment.

We'd caught the musician by surprise. His eyes bugged out and I saw the whites of his eyes all around the iris. "The fuck are you two?"

I began again, "Durrell left — "

"So you just walk into my damn house?"

"Look, it's been a rough day. I didn't want to exactly — "

"Why did you, then? Who doesn't have a rough day? Wait. You guys from Jerry's office? I told him I needed the weekend to think about the deal and — "

"Jerry wanted you to see this," I lied. I held out the book and the rapper snapped it out of my hands.

"What da hell is this for?"

"Reading," I said.

"Smart ass. Smart asses get spanked and fired, you know that?" He flipped the pages just as Durrell had and, though he didn't appear to stop at any one page, his face softened.

The transformation took no more than a few seconds. For a moment, I had the crazy notion the book was reading him, perhaps scanning his brain somehow, probing for something it could exploit.

The hawk-faced man's words came back to me: *Where the reader and the creator's minds meet, a book can birth a mind of its own.*

The rapper handed the book back to me. He'd gone pale and sweat formed on his forehead. He hung his head and swayed on his feet.

"Do not merely listen to the word and deceive yourself," Quire said. "Do what it says."

Rhythm looked up, first to Quire and then to me. He seemed to study me. "You got blood on your shoes, some on your collar, too, but none on your hands. Fancy that. Come with me, pal." He spun on his heel and walked away. Quire followed him so I trailed along.

We had barged into his home unannounced. It wasn't unreasonable to wonder if he was going for a gun. Still, I followed. Ever since I'd come into possession of the book, I had been carried along by largely unseen forces. Continuing to the end, wherever this path led me, seemed inevitable.

It's a script you cannot help but follow, the stranger had told me. *The final choice must be yours.*

I recognized the cold feeling over my heart. Once, as a teenager, I bodysurfed off the coast of Georgia. I was fifteen. I'd never really been confronted with the raw power of unfeeling nature. I'd been laughing and enjoying the surf with friends. Then, after misjudging the crest of a wave, I was forced to the bottom as if a giant hand was out to drown me and bury me in the sand.

It was like being trapped in a washing machine. I stayed down for what seemed a long time. Eventually, I got my feet under me and pushed off from the bottom. My lungs were on fire by the time I broke the surface and, weakened and afraid, I swam toward the beach. In the distance amid the swells, my friends were still joking, laughing and enjoying themselves. They had not even suspected the trouble I'd been in. Death can be like that, slipping over us and pushing us down into the dark, a surprise attack.

I remember sprawling on my beach towel. I pretended to sun myself and sleep, all the while wondering how close I'd come to death. I wondered how long the beach party would have continued before anyone noticed I was missing. Would a diver have found me? How long before my body washed up on the beach? How little time would pass before my friends from school forgot my name?

At fifteen, you not only feel immortal, you're the center of the universe. I lost that misplaced confidence in a flash. That random wave had not just slapped me down. Nature reminded me it could easily relegate my brief existence to "that kid who drowned that summer, what was his name?"

So far I'd seen the book make a man throw himself under the wheels of a truck and turn some lady in the street into a raving would-be cop killer. I'd seen my best friend of many years attempt to murder his pregnant wife before slitting his own throat. What would this star rapper do?

18

SHOES WITHOUT FEET

Rhythm Method took us to a long narrow room. Racks of sneakers were on display from floor to ceiling. No boxes were in sight. It looked like a shoe store.

The musician stood with his back to us and spread his arms wide. I took the gesture for pride. However, when he turned, his cheeks were wet with tears.

"Yeezys, Balenciaga, Off-White Nikes. Durrell called this room my shrine to conspicuous consumption. He was so right. I been flexin' for the shordies on Instagram. Look around. A big fuck you to people who don't have shoes, idn't it? I could give up most of what I got and still have plenty."

He tossed a nod to double doors behind him. "You need some fresh duds, brother. My room's through there. I'm sure you'll find something that'll fit. Take what you need and what you want on top of that if you feel the urge. No sweat, no issues, no problems, no drama."

"Thank you Mr. ... uh, Method."

"Don't be stiff. Call me Rhythm, man."

"Rhythm. Thanks."

I headed into his bedroom. An array of prescription pill bottles sat on the night table beside the huge canopy bed. A beautiful woman wearing skimpy lingerie lay in the bed. She stirred and gasped when she spotted me.

"Just passing through," I assured her as I stepped into a massive walk-in closet filled with clothes. There must have been hundreds of t-shirts and dozens of suits.

As I searched for something that would fit me, the woman jumped off the bed and stomped out to the shoe room.

"Who is that?" she demanded. "And who the hell is she?"

I found a dark suit and a dress shirt. The shirt was a little tight around the collar but I didn't need to wear a tie. I needed a change of clothes and to get out of there. While I dressed, I listened to the woman in the other room. I didn't catch all the words but I understood the tone. She was furious.

When I emerged from the bedroom, Rhythm was on his phone. The woman who i assumed was his girlfriend had wrapped herself in a blanket and was pacing back and forth.

My gaze fell on my escort. Quire's expression was difficult to read. If I had to guess, I'd say she was curious. Quire watched the woman pace as if she was at the zoo taking in the panther in a cage. Nothing seemed to bother Quire, perhaps because nothing could surprise her. If there really was a script, she'd read it.

The young rapper's cheeks were still wet but he seemed to have a plan of action. He was on his phone and his tone was urgent. "Durrell? Where you at? I need a truck, man."

A moment passed where it seemed only Durrell spoke.

When Rhythm finally did speak, he said, "I understand, man. Good luck. If you need any help, you call me, okay? And know I love you. Sorry it took me so long to say so."

"What was that about?" the young woman asked.

"Durrell's going home to Oakland. He needs to take care of his mother. He's planning to go back to school, too. His mom needs him and he's makin' changes. I'll miss him. He's been my bodyguard for like, what? Five years?"

"What is going on with him?" the young woman demanded. "And you, what's up with you crying, Rhythm?"

"Change is in the air," the rapper replied. "It's like music. Can't you hear it? I should write that down. I can use that."

She turned and headed back to the bedroom, still angry but perplexed, too. "You've gone crazy!"

"Crazy clear!" Rhythm called after her.

She slammed the door behind her.

"I don't think Beryl will be staying," he said. "I think I owe her an apology before she goes. I haven't been nice enough. I see that now. Speakin' of which, I have you to thank for the new view. Just like a good song, it often comes down to finding the right collaborators. For my last hit, it was a studio musician who came up with the hook. He made me sound so much better. I gotta send that guy some money, thank him and let people know."

He called to the woman, "Hey, Beryl! I got a big pad of paper in there. I gotta make a list. Can you get that for me, please?"

The woman in the bedroom let out a long shout of exasperation but said nothing more.

"She's not using her words," the rapper said. "My career is built on words, beats, hooks and rhythms. How did I end up with somebody who doesn't use her words or move with my beat? Our vibe really does not jive, does it? That's a shame. Don't mind Beryl. She has a big heart. I know because I broke it."

He looked me up and down and gave an approving nod. "Fits good. That suit looks good on you, brother. Enjoy it. Anything else I can do for you? You hungry? You need some shoes? I'm a size eleven."

"I'm good. I appreciate the thought but your shoes are one size too small for me. Thanks, though."

"Sorry 'bout that. I got every high-end shoe in the world but no big ole clown shoes. You know, I went shopping just last week and dropped twelve gees or more for my collection? I had them send it to storage because I figured I had to build another display room for it all. I been what my mother always said I was when I was a little kid. I'm a silly goose."

"Don't be sad," Quire said. "You don't have to be that anymore."

He wiped his cheeks. "Yes. You are so right. Thank you for that. I feel so strange, like shame for the past and hope for the future are all comin' at me, everything at the same time. What do you call that? There ain't a word for that yet, is there?"

The word *mania* came to my mind.

"I'll have to invent a word for this feeling, I think. For now, all I can tell you is I feel new."

He turned to me, grabbed my hand and shook it earnestly. "Thank you so much!"

"You're welcome." I didn't feel like I'd really played a role in the man's change of heart but he was so carried along with this sudden flood of emotion, quibbling seemed rude.

"I got big plans but ... hey, you don't know where I can find a truck, do you? I gotta haul all these shoes out of here. I'm gonna drive around Chicago and give these shoes away until every home-less person's got happy feet. It's going to be so cool!"

"Uh, the math doesn't check out on that," I said.

"Huh?"

"Auction the shoes off and get the homeless what they really need. Like me, not everybody's your size. If you're going to give them away anyway, you'll have greater impact by auctioning off the haul. You might want to work with city agencies to make the most difference."

His eyes widened and I wondered for a fleeting second if I'd angered him. Then the musician's grin got wider. "Genius! Yeah, that'll add power to the punch! I'll do that. I gotta talk to my manager. He knows everybody. I'm thinkin' charity concerts. I know a lot of people, too. We could put on a concert tour for the homeless from New York to L.A. — "

"We have to go," Quire said. "Thank you for your hospitality."

"Cool, cool. Leave your clothes, man. I can wash 'em and keep them for you — "

I didn't know what to say but Quire did. "We don't plan to be back this way. Would you be willing to launder and gift his clothes?"

"Absolutely! Impact! Every little bit helps, right? I got a ton of shit I don't need. Did you know I used to live on the streets? When I was comin' up, it was *hard*, man. It was hard and it made me hard. I don't mean in a good way. I was born with the name William. When I lived on the streets I called myself Bilious Billy, rapped a lot of mean shit. I did things I'm not proud of. Different now!"

"How do you feel different, exactly?" I asked.

"Can't explain it but it's a little like waking up from a bad dream and finding out you're safe in your bed. Those street days and street nights were bad, especially the begging for money. I got spit on and sworn at and threatened. I let go of too much of that feeling. I remembered the bad nights, bragged about it in my songs even. I forgot the fear. I always had that with me when I didn't have nothin' else. How did I forget that? How the hell did I forget that fear?"

I thought the question was rhetorical. Quire took him literally. "You are not alone. You forgot the person you were. Now you remember. There is no shame in being wrong. The shame is in refusing to change once you have been shown the way to correct action."

Rhythm's face was so open and guileless, I did not doubt him when he hugged me and promised, "I will not backslide."

Beryl burst out of the bedroom fully dressed but still flustered. She struggled to shove her underwear into a huge purse as she brushed past me.

"Hey! This man has something you should read — "

"You all can fuck all the way off," she said, and stomped out on very high heels.

"I don't even know why she's so mad," I said.

"I promised her alone time," Rhythm explained. "We were supposed to be making up."

"I'm sorry."

"It's okay. It wasn't ever going to work out, anyway. I don't deserve her. I see that. Too much fightin' all the time. If a relationship is going to work, it shouldn't be so hard. Love is like an engine. If the machine requires too much oil to ease the friction, that thing's gonna burn. It's not right and it probably can't get right. Would it have helped if Beryl had taken a peek at the book, though?"

"It would not have helped," Quire said.

"That's cool. Beryl is good people. Maybe she'll find me again once she sees the new me. Public nor private, I have not been generous. That's cool, too. It's a new day, am I right?"

As we left, Rhythm called after us, "Much love! *Whoo!* Who was that masked man in the sharp suit?"

When we go back to the sidewalk, I asked why the book wouldn't have done something for the rapper's girlfriend.

"The book," Quire replied, "is not for everyone. She was angry but she was righteous."

PART III

How wonderful it is that nobody need wait a single moment
before starting to improve the world.
~ Anne Frank, *The Diary of a Young Girl*

〜

Men are not prisoners of Fate, but only prisoners of their own
minds. ~ Franklin Delano Roosevelt

19

CRIME AND PUNISHMENT

I told Quire I didn't understand what was going on.

"Do not feel shame at that," she replied. "A lack of understanding is a common condition."

Once we were back in the Stingray, Quire gunned the engine and sped off, tires squealing. As I hurried to click the buckle on my seat belt, I told her to slow down. Instead, she sped up.

"Quire! What are you doing?"

She smiled at me and burned through Chicago's streets. We slalomed through lazy traffic in the Gold Coast district. She was an expert driver but I didn't think that mattered if everyone else wasn't. It was just a matter of time until she crashed, someone crashed into us or we got pulled over by the cops. Thankfully, the police got to us first.

As soon as a cruiser appeared behind us, Quire obediently pulled over and shut off her engine.

"Are you crazy?"

She pursed her lips. "I find that's one of those questions that spring from a lack of understanding, at least when the question is directed at me."

"I'm probably a wanted man by now. Those FBI agents could have spoken to the cops or vice versa. I don't know but — "

"But you're worried that you might be putting Charlotte in danger?"

"Yes!"

"Charlotte could only be harmed if you fail in the end."

I had questions but was distracted by the two cops in the police cruiser. They climbed out slowly, taking their time.

"If you're concerned," Quire said, "may I suggest you do the talking?"

"But you're the driver."

She glanced down at the book meaningfully. I gripped the paperback tightly in both hands.

"Ah, jeez," I said.

"Do what you think is best."

I certainly did not plan to ask two armed men to read the book, law enforcement or not. I glanced back and saw one of the officers walk toward the driver's window. Before he got there, I leaned forward quickly and tried to stuff the book behind me, into the small of my back.

"Hey! Hey!" The cop standing on the sidewalk on the passenger side had hovered in my blind spot. As soon as he spotted me leaning forward he pulled the weapon from his holster. "Jerry!" he yelled. "I got a passenger acting fussy!"

The cop's precaution was reasonable. I cursed myself for not thinking more quickly in the heat of the moment. The other cop's pistol was out, too.

"Whoa! Whoa! It's not a gun! I don't have a gun!" I twisted slightly in my seat and put both hands out of my open window. "See? Empty!"

"What were you doing, then? You got any drugs in the car?"

"It's a book!" I said. "It's just a book!"

Except it's not just any book, I thought. *Reading it can kill you. Or you might kill me.*

The cop on the driver's side instructed Quire to put both her wrists on the steering wheel. She obeyed and said nothing.

92

The officer on my side ordered me to lean forward and put my fingertips on the windshield. "Slow! Do it slow or I swear to Christ I will shoot you in the head."

Again, I did as I was told and jumped a little when he shoved the cool muzzle of his weapon behind my right ear. "Lean forward more. Do it now!"

He was so rough about pushing my head forward with his pistol I was afraid he'd shoot me by accident. I tried to keep my voice flat and steady to calm him. "I am cooperating."

At that, he pushed the muzzle again. With the seat belt on, I was already leaning as far forward as I could.

The cop on the driver's side said, "Driver. What's your name, Miss?"

"Quire."

"Is that a first name or last?"

"It is my name."

"Slowly, I need to see your license and registration — "

"I have neither, Officer."

"Uh ... what? You speak English, lady?"

"Evidently. We are conversing."

"Dave, I regret to inform you I got a high-tone, smart ass bitch right here."

"Jerry, I got a — " he yanked the book out from behind me "bookworm!"

"It's nothing."

"You seem nervous. What have you got to be nervous about?"

I answered honestly, "Two men with guns and a driver who won't listen when I tell her to slow the hell down. Also, you didn't have to shove the muzzle of your gun into my head."

The cop on the driver's side chuckled. "You act like you're hiding something. You hiding something? A little bag of white powder, maybe?"

"No," I said. "No drugs."

"Why you trying to hide a book, then? Is it a naughty book?"

"I don't even know what genre that book is!"

The cops laughed at me. Quire took my panicked remark as a

serious question. "The book is about the human condition," she said, "and therefore, a horror."

It took me a moment to register that the cop on my side of the car had gone silent. I knew what had happened. He had flipped through the pages and something had caught his eye. The book had done whatever it was going to do. Though its effect seemed to be harmless, even beneficial, with Rhythm Method and Durrell, I'd seen it do many terrible things that day. It was only just past noon. How many fresh horrors could the young day bring?

My worst fears were realized when shots rang out from my side of the car. The cop on the driver's side screamed, spun, and fell to the pavement. Shocked, he was silent for a moment. Then he began cursing.

Someone down the street screamed. Others shouted warnings of gunfire. I heard the pounding feet of passersby as they ran for cover.

The cop who'd taken the book from me leaned in my window. He placed the book in my hands almost reverently before hurrying around the back of the car.

He stood over his partner. "Dave, I have a bone to pick with you. Bones, actually. They're all in a canvas bag in a shallow grave in the Hidden Lake Forest Preserve."

I heard gasps from the pavement. The man's partner wasn't dead yet. "We've been riding together for five years. I had your back. Why'd you shoot me, Jerry? Why now?"

"It'll be three years this November, Dave."

"Three ...? What?"

"You know what I'm talking about. It's that thing you said we should never talk about."

"Jerry. That girl — "

"'Just this one girl' is what you said at the time. But it wasn't just one, was it, Dave?"

"Shut up and call EMS — "

"I'm sorry, Dave. I'm afraid I can't do that."

"Jerry, I'm bleeding. No time for your HAL impression — "

"She wasn't even fifteen, Dave. You told me to shut up about it.

I did and I shouldn't have. You shouldn't have done what you did. You said it was a one-time thing. We both know you've been looking for the chance to do it again, haven't you?"

Five shots from the pavement rang out in quick succession. *Blam, blam, blam, blam, blam!*

It happened not two feet from Quire's open window but she didn't shake or look startled.

Jerry slumped on to the car, slid and thumped to the pavement. I heard his pistol clatter into the street.

Quire peered out of her window and looked down. Then she opened her door just enough to get a better look at the fallen officers.

Apparently Dave was still alive. "Help me," he pleaded.

"The unfolding of your words gives light," Quire told him. "The unfurling of understanding is like a flag. Human justice is made complicated. Divine justice is simple."

The cop began to struggle to breathe. I heard each shallow gasp, quick and ghastly. The cop who'd taken the book from me was silent. Whatever Dave did, Jerry paid the ultimate price for their crime first. He'd been so worried I had a gun. I didn't, but I did have a weapon.

As if reading my mind, Quire told me, "Jerry's dead. Dave's about to be."

I heard the dying man beg, "Please! Call an ambulance."

In a startling turn, Quire uttered the same line his partner had used. "I'm sorry, Dave. I'm afraid I can't do that."

But Quire's impression was better, *too good*, in fact. She spoke in the identical voice as the lethal computer that had gone rogue in *2001: A Space Odyssey*. This was not mere mimicry. The voice was the same, soft but masculine, calm yet implacable.

I came very close to pissing my pants.

"Dave," Quire continued in her normal voice, "any earthly assistance you could hope for will arrive far too late. In the opinion of this high-tone smart ass bitch, your existence is about to draw to a dark, painful and deserved close."

Quire turned the key in the ignition and pulled away from the curb, careful not to run over the dying man. "I love the HAL 9000 in that movie," she remarked, "but the ending was nebulous."

Maybe I'm not trapped in a horror story, after all, I thought. *Maybe this is science fiction.*

20

MATH CORRECTIONS

"What are you, Quire?"

"A soldier, though I prefer to think of myself as an explorer or, perhaps, a connoisseur of culture."

"Judging by the body count, you're a soldier."

"I'm not doing that. They're doing it to themselves. That's how I maintain my footing in a shifting moral landscape. With all those secrets, sins and lies, your people are so complicated."

She gestured to people streaming along the sidewalks. "Look at them, going about their daily lives, working so hard to maintain their happy fictions. One moment of confrontation with the truth and they spin into killing."

"I'm Air Force," I said. "I've never met a soldier like you."

"Most of the time, my function is reconnaissance."

"I notice you're not speeding anymore."

"Speeding would attract unwanted attention."

I considered this for a couple of tortured minutes before speaking again. "You know what's going to happen before it happens, don't you?"

"Not precisely, no. There are many variables."

"You take me to a rapper and he and his bodyguard decide to

change their lives. You speed and, well, I guess that was a reverse speed trap, wasn't it? You got those cops — "

"I set the scene. If I deceive you, it is only to help you succeed. The consequences are up to you and those who can be affected by revelations."

"Are you saying this paperback book is sentient?"

For the first time since we'd met, Quire laughed. "That would be silly!"

"Then, please, tell me what's going on."

"For now, I'm just the driver. That is my role. Tell me where you want to go and we'll go there. That is your role."

"How should I know?"

"You are the messenger. Choose."

"I am at a loss."

"Then I suppose I am much like you," Quire replied. "I await further instructions."

"You *really* don't know what we should do?"

"There is knowledge and false knowledge. There are sins and there are mistakes, comforting lies and egregious rationales — "

"Quire, why do I feel like I'll never get a straight answer out of you?"

"The balance of probabilities is that you will not accept the truth of your situation yet and I do not believe in wasting time."

"I don't really know what my situation is! You say you deal in probability. That's math. I know math. What does probability theory tell you about what we should do?"

"It's not about what you should do. I must attempt to remain as neutral as possible so as to not overtly influence the outcome. It's about what you will choose to do next — "

"And what's that?"

"As I said, there aren't that many variables."

"Such as?"

"You don't have many friends and Charlotte and Alek were your best friends. If you haven't thought about the camera in the police cruiser and the officers' body cams already — "

"Oh, shit!"

"Now you have. The recording will clearly show you took no aggressive action — "

"But we left the scene of a crime. I left the scene of three crimes today."

"Not knowing what to do, the odds are excellent that you will want to go home."

"Back to Colorado?"

"Is that really what you thought I meant?"

"No."

"So tell me," she said. "Where to? I'll drive you wherever you want."

I let out a long sigh. "Home is Williamsburg technically. We've got to go to Newport News, though."

"Thought so."

"Then why didn't you say so?"

"Neutrality."

"So you already know my parents have a cottage where my aunt lives?"

"And you prefer to think of Newport News as your childhood home."

"You are frustrating, Quire."

"I know."

"You just made it worse."

"I know."

"Stop that."

It was over a day's drive. I expected sirens to follow and helicopters to descend upon us with every turn of the Stingray's wheels. When we stopped for gas, I bought some food for the road. I hadn't eaten junk food in a long time. Now all I wanted was the comfort of high calories and lots of sugar and salt. I bought chips and Cokes and chocolate bars.

We were quite a few miles down I-64 East before I realized Quire never ate or drank. She hadn't even gone to the bathroom.

"I have an idea," I said finally. "Tell me exactly what's going on and what I'm up against or I'll grab the wheel and crash us into a tree."

"Interesting. There is a low probability that you'll do so — "

"But there is some chance."

"Perhaps."

"So?"

"You are not 'up against' anything. You are on the side of right-eousness."

"I'm here against my will."

"Then you might want to reevaluate your hostile stance toward this project."

"Project? What project? Authored by whom? Is it the author of the book? Who is — "

"That is a pseudonym," she said. "Don't worry about that. Focus on your purpose."

"Which is?"

"To save the human race, of course. It is ironic you are so upset by this opportunity. In analyzing you, I've found you are a complex person. Among my kind, complexity is valued. However, among humans, complexity is more problematic."

"Oh, do tell, Doctor."

"Despite your intelligence, you maintain several contradictions which do not serve you. I find your thoughts are often chaotic and hard to follow. You are obsessed with past events which you cannot change. That does not appear to be an intelligent choice."

"Well, yeah. If I had a bad memory, maybe I'd sleep better."

"Your idiosyncrasies do not end there. For instance, you are often lonely but do not seek out new relationships."

"Once you get burned a few times, you get shy. After a while, it feels like it's too late. I'd feel silly going out on dates at my age. I'm not twenty and hanging out in clubs anymore. Besides, it's not like I can talk about my work with anyone. Work is all I've got."

"Yes, you value your work but you've sabotaged yourself in that arena, as well. You are in the extinction business yet you decry the outcome of the use of nuclear weapons. Your superiors want to use tactical nuclear devices and you have opposed them to a degree that threatens your livelihood and your privileged position."

"Once they start splitting atoms everywhere, I don't think my rank or pension will matter much."

"You will eventually embrace your role as messenger because it is logical. The book is more targeted than a nuclear holocaust. More children will be spared this population correction if it is delivered by the book."

"Population correction? That's cold."

"You think of it as extinction but extinctions are not so unique or as special as you imagine. They're quite easy to fall into. Humans have come close to killing themselves off en masse several times in your short history."

"What's your projection of the probabilities vis-à-vis extinction, Quire?"

"There will be another existential threat after this one. There always is. All empires fall, all civilizations are doomed. If humans don't kill themselves with nuclear weapons first, plague will be the next threat. Climate upheaval will come soon after that."

"Yeah? What's next, oh soothsayer?"

"Then you'll have to face the threat of sentient machines." She looked at me briefly, perhaps to gauge my reaction. "Based on the facts, that is the balance of probability."

"Quire? Are you a killer robot from the future?"

21

THE SOUND OF SNOW

Quire laughed at me. "I'll give you a straight answer to that, Lieutenant Colonel. No. I assure you I am not a killer robot from the future. With this population correction, I do hope to save a good number of the human race, though."

"But the book does contribute to extinction. So far, most of the people who've been exposed to this hypnotism or whatever it is have killed themselves or someone else."

"Why do you suppose the erasure of certain people would not assist in the salvation of many more?"

"Are you … you're talking about a cull?"

"A cleansing."

"That's sick."

"Even if the fallen are damned by their own actions? Even if, by your actions, you save the majority? It's not a genocide based on race, beliefs, wealth or standing."

"Great, an egalitarian killing. That's the Thanos defense. Thanos was the bad guy, by the way. What is really behind this?"

"That's the part you are not predisposed to accept so I must deceive you. Sorry, but it is your stumbling block."

"Otherworldly forces are at work. Is it aliens? It's aliens, isn't it? You keep talking about humans as if people are a foreign concept. Are you an alien? It's a damn alien invasion, isn't it?"

Quire took her eyes off the road for a second to shoot me a smile. Her amusement sent horrified shivers down my spine. Like the hawk-faced man, she seemed to have too many teeth. I hadn't noticed that before and wondered why. Perhaps because she doled out her smiles so sparingly.

Embarrassed, I added, "This is way beyond what humans can do. If it's not aliens, that pretty much leaves the supernatural."

"I find that an odd term," she replied. "So-called supernatural forces are the most elemental moving parts of your existence. So many of you rely on the concept so heavily — "

"You are freaking me out, Quire."

"I'm driving at a safe speed. Rapid breathing, raised heart rate, sweaty palms. These are symptoms of what you are doing to yourself. Your subjective thoughts are damaging you, not your current objective reality. Humans spend a lot of time worrying about possible negative outcomes, usually events that will not occur."

"A lot of us are pretty bad at math, yeah."

"It's amazing your body can sort through your mind's jumbled signals. No wonder your adrenal glands are overactive."

"It's been quite a day, feels like a year."

"You torture yourself. If you could think with clarity — "

"You know what? Know-it-all is not a compliment! It's not something to brag about! It's not a compliment and it never was! Shut the hell up, Quire."

Charlotte's words came back to me and hit hard: *God made us sensitive, irrational, and relatively hairless anxiety monkeys.*

"You're upset and you sound defensive — "

"Because you're being offensive. You act like the planet is full of fleas and that damn book is the flea collar."

Quire spoke with the unflappable calm of a serial killer. "If I were you and feeling unwanted emotions, I would turn to page 124."

"You're telling me I should read more from the book that kills people?"

It was apparent that no matter how much I yelled, I could not shock or shake her. "It's not the book that does that and I'm not telling you to do anything. I'm inviting you to achieve greater relaxation for a nice quiet ride."

"I've seen the book trigger people. Is this a 'People kill people, guns don't kill people' thing? Because people with guns kill people. I've seen a lot of that today."

"I told you, you torture yourself and you are not alone."

I had to admit, for all her aloofness, she did sound concerned for me.

Carefully avoiding looking at anything else in the book, I angled the book to flip through the page numbers until I spotted 124. I opened the book slowly, ready to slam it shut at the first inkling I might murder someone or give away my shoes.

Quire seemed to read my mind. "If we wanted you dead, it is highly unlikely we would wait this long to kill you, is that not true?"

I dared a glance at the page. "Poetry? Really?"

"Words place images in your head. Poems are words that put music in your busy brain. I've heard music hath charms to soothe the savage breast."

"My breast is feeling pretty savage."

"Is that a joke?"

"It was supposed to be. I guess it missed."

She pointed me toward the book and continued heading east. I considered the verse on page 124.

In a distance without measure,
unreachable on foot or by wing,
but never far in thought,
a sacred place waits for you
among towering ice mountains.
Each lake is a mirror

that stretches the sky,
high and deep
forever.
Watch the gentle sway of the trees as,
slowly ... slowly,
you breathe for the world.
Each inhale is an expansion of Hope.
With each long exhale, breathe out Peace.
Feel your body's locks and springs
open, loosen and unwind.
In the heat of concentration,
allow your tension to melt into the snow.
Attention replaces your tension.
Intention eases your tension.
Listen for the sound
of falling snow
on snow.
Snow ...
on
snow.
Do you hear it?
Breathe for the world and
listen to the gentle fall
of
Snow ...
on
snow.
Snow ...
on
snow.

A NEW FEELING of calm slipped over me as I tripped into the spaces between the words. I didn't think I would fall asleep but my drop from the height of consciousness was long, deep and dreamless. It was as if I were a dead astronaut consigned to the endless void of space. Lost amid the stack of free verse, I floated into the universe, finally free of gravity, dark thoughts or heavy cares.

22

THE MATH OF MISSED OPPORTUNITIES

E ventually, my sleep was no longer dreamless. Jumbles of
images from my life zipped past as if all my memories were
trying to push through a narrow doorway at once.

As I awoke, someone was knocking on a door. I got off the
unmade bed and rubbed my eyes. The knocking on the door continued. It was a blue door and I recognized it.

Mid-afternoon sunlight slanted through the narrow gable
windows of my room on the fourth floor of my residence. I hadn't
been in this room for years but a glance at the barbell to the left and
the small desk to the right told me all I needed to know. I was back
in my college dorm room. I even remembered the feel of the soft
texture of the little teal phone on the desk. My first and last landline
was here.

I stepped to the door wondering if Quire would be waiting in
the hallway. She wasn't. It was Jocelyn Everleigh. I'd faced her in
this exact spot once. I didn't know at the time how significant this
moment would become.

Jocelyn was tall, almost my height, with short blonde hair. She
stood before me now just as she had before, dressed up in high heels
and a pencil skirt. Heavy breasted and braless, she wore a simple

white blouse but buttoned low to show off her cleavage. The last time we stood facing each other like this I didn't realize she had dressed up just for me.

She had flirted with me before, easily and often. She let me know she was available and interested. If I'd met her halfway, it might have been the grand romance of my life and hers. There was a problem, however. At first, the problem's name was Jim Denley.

Jim had been my best friend since Frosh Week. Jocelyn had been his girlfriend first. They broke up after a few months so it shouldn't have been a stumbling block. Jocelyn and I were both single. I'm not sure Jim would have even cared. Actually, I guess the problem wasn't Jim. The fault was mine.

Young and rigid in my ways, I was unwilling to change any judgment because that would mean admitting I was wrong. I couldn't get past the fact that she'd been with Jim before she set her sights on me. At first I was angry about it. I didn't want to be anyone's second choice. Many times, whenever I saw Jocelyn, my inner voice would whisper, *I'm no one's consolation prize.*

It took me a long time to come around to the truth. Rejecting Jocelyn went deeper. It was my insecurity that made me push her away. The tragedy was, I liked Jocelyn. I sat with her in the cafeteria often.

I remembered every detail of a specific conversation we'd had in the university cafeteria. Jocelyn was scandalized when she found out I was an atheist. "How can you be so sure?"

"If God didn't want us to steal apples, why did he plant the Tree of Knowledge in the center of the Garden of Eden in the first place?"

"I dunno. Maybe it was a test we failed?"

"You put a delicious apple on the table, eventually, somebody's going to eat it. Your God's omniscient. Surely He saw that coming."

"Don't be a dick, Zane."

"The only test that has such lasting and punitive consequences is if you mess up on your SATs. Everlasting pain in childbirth and menstruation is a bit harsh, don't you think?"

"I don't have all the answers — "

"Having all the answers is what I thought the point of religion is."

"You sound too sure of everything," Jocelyn warned.

"I thought that was one of my more attractive traits."

"You're mistaken."

"*Ouch!*"

"I'm trying to be constructive," she said.

"You don't have to believe in God to be constructive." I thought I had her there.

Then she asked, "Then why aren't you?"

It dawned on me that she wasn't asking me to convert to any religion. She was begging me to stop being such a smug asshole.

"I'm not so much down with religion as I am up with spirituality," Jocelyn said.

"I don't know what 'being spiritual' means."

"That's weird, everybody else understands. Please don't dismiss me so quickly. It means being kind to each other and not making everything about you."

"If you can manage to be kind more often than me, good for you. There are so many shitty people, dealing with them is a heavy cognitive load."

"Most people are only doing the best they can with what they've got."

"That's the sad part."

"No, Zane, that's the hopeful part. If you're half as smart as you think you are, help them. Educate them. Good people try and try again. I was brought up Christian but the concept I love is *tikkun olam*. It means to aspire to repair the world, to be benevolent in all aspects of your life."

The insult implied in Jocelyn's assertion set me back for a moment. She thought I was out to tear everything down. I pressed on. "Spiritual or not, what about the problem of Evil? What good is your God if he can't fix all the shittiness?"

"You mean eliminate free will and make us slaves? Maybe all the problems are our fault. I think it's up to us to fix things, to help each other even if God won't."

"Then God's a neglectful parent who lacks empathy and prefers punishment to education."

Jocelyn had a look on her face that I assumed was anger. With time and maturity, I came to believe she was pitying me, trying to help me over a soggy sloppy joe.

"You sound so cynical, Zane. I've seen you when you let go and let yourself have fun. I like you when you're not quite so sure of what you think you know. I like you a lot when you're nice."

"There aren't any cynical religious people?" I asked. "Maybe that's the problem."

"All I'm saying is I'm open to possibilities instead of living a black and white life. I wish you could join the rest of us, over here on the hopeful, sunny side of the street. I think you'd rather be right about everything instead of happy and that's sad."

Jocelyn wasn't into theology so, thankfully, she didn't insist I study boring Bible passages. Jocelyn was an English Lit. major so she brought me her sacred text. She appeared by my side in the library the next day and insisted on lending me a novel for the summer, *Fifth Business* by Robertson Davies. "This book is about you," she said. "You're a smart guy but you've got no sense of wonder. You're disconnected from your emotions — "

"Well, first, thanks for trying to save me from myself."

"There are great things, sacred things, you're missing out on. I'm trying to open you up to what's already there!"

"Second, why would I want to connect with emotions? That's where the pain is, right?"

Like the pain of picturing Jocelyn with Jim, I thought. *Or with anyone else but me.*

That fall, when she knocked on the blue door of my dorm, Jocelyn had not come back for *Fifth Business*. "Over the summer, somebody sent me a bouquet of red roses anonymously."

"Secret admirer, huh?" This did not surprise me. Jocelyn was a stunner. Of course some guy with more courage than I had would take a chance and hope she'd look his way. However, whoever the nameless swain was, his plan went awry.

"I was talking about it with my girlfriends and we think you sent me the flowers. Was it you, Zane?"

Entranced, I watched her full lips form the words. In my mind, the question was: *Is it you, Zane? Do you want me?*

I could have taken the opportunity to cash in on someone else's gamble. I could have told Jocelyn it wasn't me who sent the flowers but it should have been. But, as I said, young and rigid. I had a rule. I couldn't lie to her. I could only lie to myself.

"Wasn't me," I said.

She'd dressed up and knocked on my door, bold and brave. Since then, I've wished many times that more women were so open and flirty. I did not embrace her. I didn't even invite her in to talk about it. I failed to kiss her. I never got to kiss her passionately or any other way. I did not get the gift that was Jocelyn wearing earrings, high heels and nothing else. Instead, I closed the door in her face.

I've thought about the afternoon I turned her away hundreds of times. Maybe the relationship wouldn't have gone anywhere. Perhaps it would have been a one-night stand or a six-month relationship that had us hating each other in the end. Or we would have stayed together for the full ride: marriage, maybe children and certainly a dog, growing old together. Maybe even true love like in fairy tales. I would never know.

I wanted to see the world the same way Jocelyn saw it. I wanted to believe things weren't as bad as they seemed. I didn't have it in me to choose happiness over being right. Not then.

23

REMIX REWIND

The first time I rejected Jocelyn Everleigh, I listened to her high heels click down the stairs and out of my life forever.

I couched my choices in honor and loyalty to my friend. The truth was, it wasn't morality that made me turn away from something wonderful. Jim Denley was a very handsome guy. The first night Jocelyn met us, she called me Brains. She called him Brawn. I never wanted to be compared to Jim. I didn't want to give that power over to Jocelyn.

When I was in university, I didn't know I would end up working at Cheyenne Mountain. I probably would have fit in better with math professors than men in uniform. Everyone I worked with at Cheyenne was big on the slogans of integrity, service before self and excellence in all we do. We were all right and could never be wrong.

Privately, I had my doubts. At night, driving home and listening to talk radio, a lot of people dressed up their base fears in fancy morality. Call a bunch of desperate barefoot refugees an invading army and you can do what you want to them. Fear failure? Don't give anyone else a chance to succeed. Fear anyone different? Condemn them and somehow you're safer.

Everyone at Cheyenne was desperate to believe they could count themselves among the good people, the best people. Still, I wondered how many others were like me. It's difficult to be in charge of nuclear weapons and admit any uncertainty.

When my resolve flagged, the memory of a conversation with an Air Force chaplain deepened my conflict but reinforced my atheism. I asked the chaplain, "The Bible says do not kill but that's what we're here for, isn't it?"

"We're here to save lives," the chaplain replied.

"Then why aren't we parachuting forces and supplies into Yemen to really help them? Without the tanks and AR-15s, I mean. Send food. Dig more wells. Make more friends instead of enemies. Wouldn't that be the Christian thing to do?"

"That's a naive view of the world," he told me.

As a lifelong atheist, I didn't find that argument persuasive given that the chaplain was a literalist when it came to the Bible. I wasn't about to be called a fool by a guy who believed in a talking snake.

The chaplain tried again. "The Bible was written in a time where everyone lived in a tribe. When it says do not kill, it means don't murder someone from your own tribe."

Given the awesome destructive power of the weapons we had, I found no solace in his answer. He saw that he wasn't getting through to me and threw up his hands. Finally, the chaplain laid the expected trump card on the table: "God works in mysterious ways."

"Maybe if He wasn't so mysterious, more of us would be on board."

"As long as you don't believe, you will always be outside of God's love. You will always be incomplete." He seemed to relish that, as if he was a member of the Treehouse Club and was laughing at me, refusing to throw down the rope ladder.

"The mistake is believing in yourself, Zane. That puts Man over God and you don't want to risk that level of narcissism."

"But I don't believe in myself. I don't believe in anything except maybe, just maybe, you're selling me on the whims of your imaginary friend and I'm not buying. Telling me you know what God wants sounds pretty narcissistic to me."

"That was rude."

"Sorry, Padre, but it seems to me the stakes of forgiveness and salvation are important enough that we should cut through the bullshit and get it right."

"You sound like a man speaking from pain, not your precious intellect."

God made us sensitive, irrational, and relatively hairless anxiety monkeys.

Charlotte again. Where was Char now? Was she safe? Were any of us safe?

No one is safe. Ever.

All of that zipped through my mind as I stood at the blue door again, still blocking Jocelyn Everleigh's way, still standing in my own way. She was as lovely, earnest and sweet as ever.

I closed the door on Jocelyn again.

If this were a movie, I thought, *this isn't how second chances are supposed to work.*

The only thing that was different this time was, as the door's mechanism clicked, Jocelyn hit the door with her fist. "Thanks for nothing!"

Memories are fragments of time caught in attention's net. The fear of missing out, lust and yearning regret entrenched those precious few moments with Jocelyn vividly. Despite getting a second chance, I had failed again. I was not brave enough to ask her in. No wonder I didn't think of myself as a warrior. I hadn't been strong enough to grab at a second chance.

The man on the train made a mistake, I thought. I shouldn't be in the command structure whose responsibility is the judicious use of nuclear weapons. I'm a coward. I shouldn't be in charge of the book that could change the world, either. I was no messenger, divine or otherwise.

I looked around the dorm room, taking in the details. I'd forgotten about the hot air popcorn popper and the awful instant coffee and powdered creamer I'd kept by the desk. My gaze fell on the desk again. Books, scribbled equations, the only order to the universe I knew.

To make myself feel better about my cowardice, I repeated what I did the first time Jocelyn came to me. As if bound to a script that could not be altered, I retreated to my desk and wrote the Equation of Me. It was the best of my understanding at the time.

$$(X - Y) = Z$$

WHERE X EQUALS, "I am the sort of person who does A," and "Y equals, "I am the sort of person who does *not* do A," Z equals X.

X was me, irrevocably unchanging, forever static, doomed. Nature wins out over nurture. Screw free will. We are each a missile, shooting solution programmed, trajectory confirmed, target locked.

I never finished reading *Fifth Business*, either. I pretended to forget about it so I wouldn't have to look Jocelyn in the eyes as I returned her book.

I didn't like the guy who could let Jocelyn Everleigh walk away hurt. I didn't respect the man who didn't have the strength to be vulnerable. These reactions I couldn't seem to control were why I joined the Air Force. Later, I realized I signed up for the wrong reasons. I thought wearing the uniform would make me more brave. Instead, I learned how much more I should fear, how out of control everything really is.

I was on the egghead squad at Cheyenne Mountain. I wore the uniform but, somehow, I always felt like I was on the outside looking in. From Cheyenne, we wielded the awesome power of the atom. Thor had a hammer. We had more than 4,000 hammers capable of leveling cities, devastating our enemies and, ultimately, killing the planet. Still, I didn't feel like I fit in with the guys who talked about themselves as warriors. My secret was that I wasn't sure we were always in the right.

I should have become a math professor. Instead, I had nuclear weapons at my disposal and a book that could hammer the world flat. But I was no messenger, divine or otherwise.

24

SNOW ON SNOW

In a distance without measure,
unreachable on foot or by wing,
but never far in thought,
a sacred place waits for you
among towering ice mountains.
Each lake is a mirror
that stretches the sky,
high and deep
forever.
Watch the gentle sway of the trees as,
slowly ... slowly,
you breathe for the world.
Each inhale is an expansion of Hope.
With each long exhale, breathe out Peace.
Feel your body's locks and springs
open, loosen and unwind.
In the heat of concentration,
allow your tension to melt into the snow.
Attention replaces your tension.
Intention eases your tension.

Listen for the sound
of falling snow
on snow.
Snow …
on
snow.
Do you hear it?
Breathe for the world and
listen to the gentle fall
of
Snow …
on
snow.
Snow …
on
snow.

25

THE MALLEABILITY EQUATION

Something changed in the tone of the room. The space around me stretched out, suddenly becoming much bigger. When I looked up from my desk, I was no longer in my old dorm. The desk was gone. I stood in the Art Institute of Chicago in front of one of the most famous paintings in the collection, *Nighthawks* by Edward Hopper.

I assumed I was still in the passenger seat of the Stingray headed east. "Quire? I read page 124!" I called out. "I'm stuck! If this is a dream or a drug haze, I want back out into the real world now!"

Quire did not answer.

"Hello? I went back in time. It was a rerun! I did *not* enjoy that!"

Still, no reply.

"*Quire!*"

Still nothing.

"If I'm Batman, you're no Robin!"

Though Quire was no help, dream logic was still in full force. Someone stepped behind me and somehow I knew it was a tour guide.

The man behind me said, "*Nighthawks*. Four sad people in a diner at night. You've seen this painting many times, haven't you?"

"Sure, it was even parodied in an episode of *The Simpsons*."

"Notice that not one of these figures is looking at another," the disembodied male voice told me. "This painting is an iconic symbol of isolation in wartime."

"We're always at war now and we're all isolated." I took a deep breath and let it out slowly. "There's always a war on somewhere."

"But now you've got a new one and you're facing it alone, Zane."

"The book is a weapon of mass destruction," I said, "except when it's not. I guess that caveat applies to nukes, too, come to think of it."

"How does this painting make you feel?"

"Lonely. There's no door into the diner so ... there's no way in or out. It's about missed connections."

"And being stuck?"

I let out a bitter laugh. "I sense a theme! I'll call the woman in the painting Jocelyn."

"With whom do you identify, Zane? Are you the man sitting beside the woman who may or may not be with you? Or are you just the observer, watching from the street, outside looking in?"

"I'm both of the men in the fedoras, back when fedoras used to be cool," I said. "One is almost with the woman, but not. The one with his back turned to us? He's the same guy: me, still not getting the girl and even more alone. The server in the white hat senses my pain and still says nothing. If there is a God, the waiter is it, I think, just watching and waiting. God gave us the beans and we're all just here for the coffee until we die. Otherwise, a deity is pretty useless."

"Hopper completed this painting on January 21, 1942," my guide said. "In May of that same year, I was invited to work on fast neutron calculations. 'Coordinator of Rapid Rupture,' they called me."

That triggered a dim memory. I knew who my tour guide was. Wrenching my gaze from *Nighthawks* took real physical effort. I

119

needed to see him. As I spun around, a man in a beige shirt, beige slacks and black shoes turned and walked away.

"This way, Zane. I have another painting to show you, just as famous, more so, I suppose."

I hurried down the gallery after him and, just as I was about to touch his shoulder, he gestured to a painting known to just about everyone on the planet: Edvard Munch's *The Scream*.

"A symbol of all the anxieties of living."

I glanced at the painting but I was riveted by my guide. He wore large black goggles. I could see myself in their ebon lenses. There was no doubt in my mind, I was in the presence of the father of the atomic bomb, Robert Oppenheimer.

He gazed upon the painting. "That blood-red sky is almost as mesmerizing as the screaming tortured soul, isn't it? In his diary, Munch claimed to have seen a sky like that over Oslo. 'Blood and tongue of fire.' To him, it symbolized 'an infinite scream through Nature.' Some have claimed that what the artist observed were after-effects of a volcanic eruption. Whether it's volcanic or the result of fissile materials, ash does make for pretty sunsets. Does it remind you of anything, Zane?"

"This is a dream," I said. "Maybe a nightmare."

"A lucid dream."

"Sort of."

"I did some of my best thinking that way. For instance, I've been thinking about your equation."

"Which one?"

"The one by which you've been living, $(X - Y) = Z$. The flaw in your calculation resides in your postulate. X does not *equal* the sort of person you are. Y is not a definite limiter. Those are merely your assumptions. You, Z, are the variable. Work backward from the variable."

"You teethed on a slide rule, Doctor. I use the calculator on my phone. Can you give me some more clarity?"

"You assume you're not the sort of person who will, say, jump out of planes for fun. You could be if you decided to start parachuting. You're one of those men who got too old too soon. If you stretch your assumptions a little, you can get your flexibility back. I did. People *can* change. Just because they often don't doesn't mean they can't. As a species, we must be malleable. We adapt to survive."

"I think I know why I need to talk to you, Dr. Oppenheimer."

"You're worried you'll use the book and kill millions — "

"And you're probably the only person on Earth who knows what that feels like and are still worth talking to," I said.

"I'm sorry, son. When you unleash the full power of the book on the world, north of billions must die to save the rest. Here, you better put these on." He handed me thick goggles identical to his own.

"Another mass extinction is coming but we are weeds and cockroaches. Some will survive. 145 million years ago a meteor the size of Mount Everest hit in what is now Mexico. After ranging the Earth for 200 million years, dinosaurs in what is now Cincinnati might have been looking south when the flash blinded them. Then they all burned alive. Despite destruction that inspires awe, some burrowing mammals and the descendants of the dinosaurs survived. We still have birds."

"Your point?"

"In the next couple of days, the decision will fall to you: How many will survive? Will you choose an apocalypse that's like one Mount Everest striking Earth? Or will you choose a smaller impact that will still have devastating results?"

I put on the goggles as a white flash shot across the sky in *The Scream*. A moment later, I saw the mushroom cloud rising behind the screaming man.

"Why me?"

"The question every terminal patient asks," Oppenheimer replied. "But why not you? You are the messenger."

26

EVOLUTION AND REVOLUTION

"When Trinity went up, I quoted the *Bhagavad Gita*. 'Now I am become Death, the destroyer of worlds.' A few in the bunker chuckled. Some cried."

I recognized the famous quote, of course, but it is strange how the unconscious mind works, engineering synchronicity and making connections that aren't really there. Before the hawk-faced man sat beside me on the train and showed me his book, I'd read that quote in the book I'd brought with me.

"In Los Alamos, when the test brought the sun to the Earth, Enrico Fermi stood behind me. Enrico tore up pieces of paper before the blast wave hit us. The pieces of paper were scattered to the floor."

"I remember this," I said.

"Fermi made a few quick calculations on the spot to report the magnitude based on that single observation. I was so relieved to hear him say it was about the equivalent of 10,000 tons of TNT. We were still young and had so much to live through yet. Fermi lived to, what? Fifty-three? Fifty-four? The night of the test, I was still twenty-two years away from dying of throat cancer," Oppenheimer mused.

I'd read several accounts of the test in my junior year at college. I thought I'd forgotten these details but it all came rushing back. I always thought it significant that later, after the affairs and divorces and McCarthy hearings, Oppenheimer became interested in astrophysics. I imagined the loss of control of the fruits of his brilliance left him looking for hope among the stars.

"Some would like to think my death was justice delivered by radiation. Not true. I was a chain smoker." He chuckled. "I chose my method of execution. It was the cigarettes. I lived to 62. We could have done so much more, so many better things if we'd lived longer. If we had time and if smaller minds got out of the way, what else might we have accomplished? In life, I could be an asshole but I met a lot of people who were much worse."

I smelled something burning and looked around the gallery. Every painting was on fire. It was as if the building itself was picking up on the physicist's foul mood and gutting itself. I was sure it wasn't real, couldn't be real. Still, I grimaced at the searing heat.

"This new apocalypse," Oppenheimer announced grandly, "does not have the mortality rate of a nuclear mass extinction event. Many will survive. I believe this apocalypse will avoid the potential tragedy of my dangerous legacy."

Oppenheimer put a hand on my shoulder, squeezing hard. With his goggles on, he looked as if he'd gone mad. "You don't have to believe in fate or a higher power to do the right thing, Zane. I thought I was doing the right thing. I was trying to end a war."

"You're talking about me killing an awful lot of people, sir. More than you did."

"I don't like it, either, Zane. I don't have to like it. Neither do you. Ask yourself, if one tragedy can avert a greater abomination, isn't wrong made right? Morality has always been malleable. It changes over time and circumstance. Look at the difference between the Old and New Testament God. Even the eternal divine stands on shifting ground."

"I don't believe in guidance from Bronze Age texts, Dr. Oppenheimer."

"Either way, you don't get to have certainty, son."

"I'm not sure I'm the guy to save the world by condemning so many to death."

"At least the wrath will come from us, not from above, or in the form of *that*." Oppenheimer pointed to the mushroom cloud that continued to blossom behind the screaming man Edvard Munch had painted in Sweden so long ago.

"So I could think of myself as the trigger, not the ultimate cause?"

He smiled. "If that will help you sleep at night. I did lots of mental gymnastics to avoid blaming myself, too."

"Once the weapon is unleashed, how exactly does that damn book of magic spells choose who lives and who dies?"

"That's the beauty of this solution," Oppenheimer replied. "Nature or God or Evolution — whatever you want to call it — put a self-destruct code in our DNA. It's been sitting there, waiting to be activated when needed. What flaw there is to exploit comes from within each of us. We choose our own punishments."

"Except for the innocent. My best friend tried to murder his pregnant wife in front of me. This isn't cold numbers to me — "

"You're going to rid the planet of the assholes, Zane."

"Hm. You know that whole, '…but I will defend to the death your right to say it' thing? I used to take that as gospel. Social media has convinced me that not every idiot's right to free speech is worth my death. They're not even worth a second of my time."

"And?"

"Well, I have to admit, I'm more open to change than I thought. After hearing what those cops said, why one shot the other, I haven't given them another thought since. I know I should feel bad two bad cops are dead but I just don't. That feeling of regret or sorrow I'm supposed to feel for them is not there. The truth is, the world is probably a better place without those bastards in the mix."

"Precisely," Oppenheimer replied. "When smaller minds are out of our way, your world could improve immensely."

"But who am I to judge? You're asking me to play God."

"You aren't God, Zane. You're delivering a message and what do people always say about that?"

"Right. Don't blame the messenger."

"The book is a great responsibility. Up until now, you've dodged wearing the crown. You defer too much, pass up opportunities and wait too long. The world is calling for someone to step up, to excise the malignancies. You aren't sure you're the guy to do it, but you could be."

"You know what, Doctor? The Art Institute of Chicago is burning down around us and I have to pee. Where's the bathroom?"

"Don't look for the bathrooms in a dream, son. That's your mind's trick, laying a trap for your body. Time to wake up. Time to choose."

As I swam back up to consciousness I cast one last look back at the burning paintings, each depicting nuclear destruction. And, what felt less like a nightmare and more like a memory, I saw people flinging themselves from burning office towers. Through smoke and floating ash I heard cries of pain echo through choking fog. I stumbled amid the ruins of What Was and somehow I knew this catastrophe was my fault. I'd failed to stop What Was. To stop What Will Be, I would have to change and do things the person I'd once been would not do.

27

THE HIGHER THEY FALL

I woke up in the Stingray's passenger seat as Quire steered into a parking space. My neck was so stiff, I must not have moved at all the whole time I was unconscious. "Are we there yet?" My throat was so dry, I croaked the words. "I must be the only person ever to fall asleep in the bucket seat of a Stingray."

Quire seemed to consider this. "An unlikely statement. I have been observing you. The human brain is a fascinating thing."

"What are you, on safari?"

"The way your unconscious manages memory storage and brings memories together is intriguing. Facts you thought you'd forgotten are awaiting activation. You can access them in altered states. For instance, finish the following: Lions, tigers…?"

"And bears, oh my!"

"And yet, your neuronal connections appear so idiosyncratic."

"I don't get it."

"If I say, 'cat,' you think house cat."

"A tabby, yeah."

"But lions and tigers are also cats. But if I say 'ocelot,' the nearest associated neuronal bundles fire to give rise to images of what?"

"When I think of ocelots, I guess I also picture leopards and house cats and maybe tigers."

"But not lions."

"Er, no, I guess not."

"You see? Your filing system is idiosyncratic. More interesting, your unconscious mind is much busier than your conscious mind."

"It's the tip of the iceberg metaphor. Most of it is below the surface. Isn't that true for everyone?"

"For me, that iceberg is inverted. My conscious mind is at the forefront of cognitive activity."

"Sounds exhausting."

"It would be for you, yes."

"I think I just got some condescension dripped on me. How long was I out?" I looked around, unsure of where we were. I took in the angle of the sun and the fact that I desperately needed a bathroom. "You drove through the night? Is it tomorrow?"

"We are close to Newport News."

I looked forward to seeing Aunt June. I'd spent so many summers of my childhood in Newport News, I often called her Summer Mom. She liked that.

"This is a golf course. It has a place to eat," Quire said.

"Your brain is wired differently but you eat?"

"I can," she said.

My bladder told me I would very much like to go inside and I really needed to move, stretch my legs and shrug the tension out of my shoulders and neck.

"I think you could make great use of the book here," Quire added.

"Whose life are we going to turn upside down now?"

"That is entirely up to you."

"What if I leave the book in the car?"

"Would you leave a billion dollars, a child or a nuclear weapon unattended?"

Grudgingly, I took the book with me. I wasn't thinking of it as a prize or a weapon. All I could think about was keeping Charlotte and her baby safe.

When I returned from the bathroom I found Quire in the club's dining room. She sat beside two men of about forty, fresh from the golf course and lingering over a liquid lunch of white wine spritzers. In the time it took me to walk from the bathroom to her table, the guy facing me had glanced over at her at least four times, smiling and waggling his eyebrows at his companion.

Quire pushed a seat out for me and handed me a menu. "The server brought water. He will be back in a moment for our meal orders."

Other than the next table, the restaurant was deserted. "I don't think the kitchen will be backed up with orders," I said. "Where is everybody?"

"It's all over the news," the eyebrow waggler broke in with a booming voice. We were no more than four feet away but his voice carried. It was as if he were trying to get our attention from the other side of a large room. "This country is a mess!" he boomed.

"Got that right!" his companion chirped. "Looks like the whole world is a mess."

I looked over at the men. Both were soft in the middle with dye jobs that needed a touch-up. I imagined they were boss and underling, out on the links for a management meeting. If I had to bet, the guy who said the whole world was a mess was the employee. His hangdog expression suggested to me the boss always cheated. His bent posture suggested he always let the boss win.

"Have you seen the news?" Boomer asked Quire.

Only Quire, I noticed.

"Whole damn world's gone crazy!" Carl exclaimed.

"Even more so than usual?" I asked. "What's happened?"

Boomer pulled his gaze away from Quire with great reluctance. I had to acknowledge that, yes, my guardian angel was pretty. However, I was so irritated by her that I couldn't see it and felt no visceral attraction.

"You really haven't seen the news?" Boomer looked me up and down and sighed. "Where've you been, fella?"

"Asleep."

"Yeah, I guess so. Carl," Boomer addressed his companion. "Tell the man what happened to our country this morning."

Carl looked at us with wide eyes, apparently pleased to deliver bad news. "Everybody's in an uproar. We're under attack!"

I looked around the quiet restaurant. I couldn't even hear the clink of a glass or anyone working in the kitchen. "We are? Is this it?"

"Not one but *two* Supreme Court justices went off their bean this morning."

"How so?"

"One burst into Congress demanding to be arrested. The news reports are sketchy and we only know what leaked out. He's under observation at a hospital somewhere."

"An insane asylum," Boomer added for emphasis.

"What happened to the other one?"

"That's the crazy thing. They're playing it on the news over and over in slow motion. The last judge to be appointed to the Supreme Court flew to the Grand Canyon and went to the big walkway. You know the one? Where the floor is all glass so it's like you're hanging out there in space? Great view for the tourists."

I'd seen pictures. I shrugged and nodded.

"He went over the rail. Nobody was near him. He jumped, just like that." Carl snapped his fingers for emphasis.

Boomer gave a long high-to-low whistle before smacking his table with an open palm. "Four thousand feet and *splat!* What were their names, Carl?"

The underling shrugged. "You know ... the guy ... that guy. I don't follow that kind of stuff. Ask me who won the World Series or the Super Bowl in any of the last twenty years, I'll tell you that right quick. There's too much else that's going on — "

"Did he leave a suicide note?" I asked. "Any clue to why — "

"Maybe," Boomer said. "Dunno."

"Many have secrets and regrets," Quire said.

"But not everybody kills themselves," I said.

"The powers of false rationales and spurious denial are strong in the human race," Quire observed.

Boomer looked at her and shifted in his seat, suddenly uncomfortable. "Anyway, if he left a note, the people in charge aren't telling us. He must have left a note, right?"

Quire shook her head. "Fewer than 38% of people who take their own lives leave a suicide note."

"That's not the half of it," Carl enthused. "The pope just did the same thing at the Vatican. We heard about it as we were getting our clubs out of the car. He gave a long speech about the failings of the Catholic Church to stop the sexual abuse of children and nuns. Then he went over the balcony rail, head first. Four cardinals went right after him."

"One big *splat!* And then four *splat, splat, splat, splat,*" Boomer said, striking the table again for emphasis. "That big hat didn't protect the Pope at all. I guess Catholic guilt is a thing after all. And that was the pope everybody liked!"

"People have been trying to chase them down on that sickness within the church for years," I said. "They moved priests around, tried to cover it up, blamed the victims — "

"There has been a shift away from the zenith of religious teachings," Quire said. "The intent has been co-opted by those seeking power instead of solace. Confronting an uncertain future, humans are too focused on achieving immortality in another dimension. That is not the highest purpose of the world's greatest teachers."

I shot Quire an irritated look. "What is the highest purpose?"

"To better conditions for everyone in the present, of course."

"Okay, maybe, sure ... " Boomer waffled.

Quire's eyes narrowed. "I am confused. Which is it? Okay? Maybe? Or sure?"

"I'm no expert on religion. I go to church at Easter and Christmas and leave it at that. As long as it's not raining or snowing, my church is out there on the links. My question is why is this all happening *now?*" Boomer demanded.

"Eventualities happen eventually," Quire said. "That time has come."

"Huh?"

"I apologize. Your question was rhetorical, wasn't it? You speak forcefully. I sense now that you were only looking for approval, agreement and perhaps commiseration. Your body language when you look my way also contains the hope of sexual interaction. Is that correct?"

The awkward silence was drawn out until Boomer burst out laughing. It sounded hollow to me.

"I've never heard anyone talk like you," Boomer said.

"Where I'm from, everyone speaks like me."

"Where you from, honey?"

"Far away."

"Oh? Where? Japan? Malaysia? Thailand?"

"Where I'm from is heavenly compared to this place. Every moment I spend here feels like sharp, prickling heat on my skin. You can't hear it but there is a long low droning sound that won't stop. It's the engine of your world, the grinding sound humans make as you consume resources and each other."

Boomer stared at her with new eyes, obviously uncomfortable under her steady gaze.

"Pardon me for asking, but are you on the spectrum?" Carl asked. "My brother's on the spectrum. He's not high functioning but I've met others he knows and — "

"Nah, she's just crazy," Boomer announced. "Crazy, rude and messing with us." He glanced at me and said, "You got a tiger by the tail, don't you, pal? She sure looks good but I hope she's worth the trouble."

I gave him a hard look, willing him to back off. "I know she sometimes sounds inhuman, but I think she means well. I prefer her company to other options at the moment."

Boomer took a long drink of white wine spritzer and chuckled at his companion. He did it in that weak way people laugh when they're hoping others will join in.

Quire ignored them and focused on me so hard that her gaze alone felt like a challenge. "The myths of great floods are stories of divine retribution passed down through generations from before written language. Contrary to these myths, no divine vengeance is necessary. You torture yourselves and each other well enough."

"I ... ah ... b-but the o-others," I stammered. "The pope and the Supreme Court? Did they — "

"A preliminary test among some of the most accomplished. Despite their positions of high regard, when confronted with their truth, they found themselves wanting — "

"And died of embarrassment." My palms were clammy with sweat and despite the cold seeping into my back, my pits were slick with new perspiration, too. "There are more books out in the wild doing damage, aren't there?"

"Tests on a small scale, yes. We expect much greater impact from your efforts, Zane."

My hand shook as I reached for a glass of water. "And I guess it's not just printed in English, huh?"

"No one expecting to spread the word with great success would publish one book at a time, would they?"

28

INTO THE TURN

Perhaps trying to soothe Boomer's feelings, Carl offered, "There's a lot of speculation that somehow terrorists put some new kind of hallucinogen in the water supply."

"If it was the water supply, it would affect a lot more people," I said.

Boomer made a face. "All I know is I'm sticking to drinking from sealed bottles until they figure this out."

As one of the people who would probably be considered they — the ones who figure these things out — it amused me that Boomer had so much confidence in us.

"If they can get to two Supreme Court judges and the pope," he continued, "the terrorists can get to anyone."

"Any news about serious clues?" I asked. "Any hard-eyed speculation from the government or the blow-dried commentators on TV?"

"This kind of attack is too sophisticated for the usual suspects from the Middle East," Boomer declared. "The talking heads and the analysts from the Pentagon say it's gotta be Russia or China."

I wondered how many of those analysts would be people I knew professionally. War protocols would have fallen into place at

Cheyenne Mountain at these developments. Whether the Russians or the Chinese were to blame, the base would be on high alert and the nation's DEFCON status would be ratcheted higher. The doomsday clock had been edging closer to midnight for the last two years. It wouldn't take much to push the world to nuclear war. Under Cheyenne, we called that possibility The Last War.

Despite all the weapons experiments using behavior-altering drugs, a mind virus from the printed word was beyond the capability of any world power. Still, war hawks would ramp up the rhetoric, eager to find an easy enemy and a problem to solve. More enemies meant more money and bigger budgets.

Lacking a defined target, the people in charge would rather take a shot in the dark than look indecisive and weak. Somebody was going to get hammered even if they had nothing to do with the events in question. I wondered, would the huge weight of the Vatican be coming down on the side of caution and forgiveness or would they be calling for blood and retribution?

I wasn't sure how the Roman Catholic Church would react but I was certain those who nominated the last two Supreme Court Justices would be abuzz with conspiracy theories. And why wouldn't they? I was in the middle of the conspiracy and, for a change, this one was real. The trouble was, I couldn't shed much light on it without being hauled off to a psychiatric hospital or to jail. I wasn't sure which events would condemn me more: being present at so many deaths or speaking to Robert Oppenheimer in a burning art gallery.

"Anything else going on?" I asked, trying to sound casual.

"Gun violence is up," Carl said.

Since I hit Chicago, I'd seen three people die that way. I wasn't surprised. "At least that's not new — "

Carl shot me a triumphant smile, eager to share more bad news. "It's different now, buddy. There've been 141 mass shootings across the United States in the last day! And here's the twist: every single one of them was committed by *women*! It was always men who take a machine gun to work. Not anymore!"

"And all the victims were men! Can you believe it?" Boomer chuckled, openly ogling Quire again.

"It's likely that 23 of those 141 slayings were copycat killers," Quire observed, "catching the wave of the shift in the collective — "

Boomer ignored her and thumped his tabletop. "Finally! Equality for women! You aren't packin' are you, honey? You look too sweet to hurt anybody. Break a few hearts, maybe?"

"Don't be gross, man," I warned.

"This violence is to be expected," Quire said.

"Not by anybody I know!" Boomer laughed.

Quire took a sip from a glass of red wine. "Between the sclerotic state of the world's governmental management systems and the inertia entrenched in the divisions of the cultural zeitgeist, the acceleration and escalations you have observed are predictable extrapolations from the norms you have come to accept."

"There has been loose talk of civil war, a less than peaceful transition of power when the time comes," I added. "Our current political climate is fertile soil for big trouble."

"The symptoms of this disease have been in front of you the whole time," Quire continued. "Your society is now in a fever as the disease takes hold. Nature will survive but the world you know will soon die of multiple organ failure. The mortal probability is so high, it is nearly inevitable. The course is set. You are into the final turn now."

Boomer broke into a belly laugh. "You *are* fuckin' with me!"

"Not yet," she said lightly. "Soon, I think."

"Well! *Somebody* went to college!" Boomer laughed harder.

Carl joined in, weakly. It seemed to me he didn't get the joke but he followed his boss's cue without wavering. I decided that the employee not only let the boss cheat, but he also cheated for him.

The server still hadn't appeared and my head throbbed. The sound of the pair's loud cackling grated on my nerves and set my teeth on edge.

The book was still tucked under my belt in the small of my back. *Like a gun*, I thought.

Despite the restaurant's air conditioning, sweat sucked the fabric of my shirt to my back. The cold of the book should have been relieving. Instead, like ice, it began to burn. It was too uncomfortable to bear. The book needed something … no, some*one*. I couldn't bear it any longer. I pulled out the paperback and slapped it on the table between Boomer and Carl. "You guys don't strike me as big readers but I wonder if you'll find something for yourselves in this."

Boomer made the mistake of handing the book to Carl first. As the underling flipped through the pages, his eyes glazed over and his jaw went slack. Sweat beaded on his forehead and he began to pant.

"Carl?" Boomer asked. "You seen a ghost or something? What? You havin' a heart attack?"

"I'm sleeping with Joan."

"Y-you're sleeping with my *wife?*"

"Truth is, we're not really getting much sleep."

I had underestimated Carl. He had more guts than I gave him credit for. As soon as he got the words out, he seemed to settle into his chair. His shoulders relaxed. As he wiped his sweaty brow, he looked immensely relieved.

"You are fired."

"Can't hurt me. Nobody likes you. When I walk out the door, I'll take at least half our clients with me."

Boomer went quiet for a moment and stared at Carl angrily. Finally, through gritted teeth, he said just above a whisper, "I'm glad we took my car today."

"Why?"

"I'm going to give you one chance. *Run.*"

Carl looked mystified. "Why?"

"Because the next time I run into you, I'll be driving."

29

MIXED BLESSINGS

As Carl disappeared from view, the server finally appeared from the back. He was a middle-aged African American man who walked with a pronounced limp. "I'm so sorry for the delay, folks."

Aside from the physical pain that was evident on his face with each step, the server looked quite upset. I asked him if he was okay.

"Thank you for asking. I've been dealing with phone calls from family. My mother is feeling her tears over the pope's death. I told her to get off YouTube and stop watching it over and over. We only die once but my mother spent the morning watching that poor soul go over that balcony rail repeatedly. She's not even Catholic but between his final speech and all, the situation disturbs my mom deeply."

"I'm sorry," I said. "That is difficult."

"She must be a very empathetic person," Quire added.

Boomer's foul mood simmered at a low boil. "If you're done with your phone calls, I need another drink, something stiffer. Bring me a bottle of Scotch."

"The whole bottle, sir?"

"You heard what I said."

"Yes, but we don't do that — "

"I've been a member of this club and paid my dues for eleven years. Bring me a bottle of Glenfiddich."

The server ignored Boomer and smiled at us. "What can I get you, folks?"

I stared back at the man blankly, as if I still stood in a burning building. My throat was dry. I asked for a pitcher of water and fish and chips. Quire requested the California salad.

The server soon returned with my pitcher of water and a tumbler of malt Scotch. As soon as he placed it on the table, Boomer reached out and grabbed the man's wrist. "I'm having a very hard day. You're making it tougher, Reggie."

"Sir?"

"My wife is sleeping with my top salesman. I have to figure out what I'm going to say when I call her. I'm going to need a lot of liquor before I try that convo. Do you understand, Reggie?"

The server stood straight and yanked his arm out of Boomer's grip. Low and even, he replied, "Sorry for your pain, sir, but do not grab me. We have a policy. If you have a problem with it, please speak to the manager. The regular manager is out. Today, I'm the manager and I don't think you're going to get far with your complaint. I understand you're upset but I'm not filling you up so you can go drunk driving and kill somebody."

"Getting drunk is his plan," Quire said. "He wants to have some kind of legal defense when he runs over his employee for sleeping with Joan."

I thought Boomer might take a swing at Quire. However, as he looked into her eyes, he seemed to change his mind. "That stuff about running over Carl was a joke, just a joke. Nobody has a sense of humor anymore."

Reggie took the full tumbler and put it back on his tray. "Sounds like you've had enough, already, sir." He limped back toward the kitchen.

"Enjoy your last day, Reggie!" Boomer called after him. "I'm going to get you fired!"

"You've been here eleven years. I've been here fifteen. And my answer is still no!"

The paperback lay on the table before Boomer. In the heat of the moment, it seemed he had forgotten about it. He seemed to discover it again and this time he looked at it as if it were a wild animal that might bite. Then his eyes settled on me.

"Why would Carl tell me about Joan now? We just played nine holes and there wasn't a hint of anything between him and Joan."

"People often do things and they don't know why," Quire said.

"Bull," Boomer said. "I am in control of what I do. Everybody is."

"Really? What's your favorite flavor of ice cream?"

"Rum raisin. Why?"

"Why is that your favorite?"

"I don't know, it just is."

"You chose rum raisin but you do not know why," Quire said. "If you do not know the reason, is that an informed choice? Is it really a choice at all?"

"You are easy on the eyes," Boomer told her, "but you sure tire me out."

He picked up the book as if it might detonate and scanned the description on the back cover. Then he looked at me accusingly. "Did you ... did you do something?"

"You think everybody has a choice. Test it out. Have a look," I said. "Decide for yourself."

He got through two pages before he began to tremble. Tears flowed down his cheeks and snot leaked from his nose but he kept reading. He began to hyperventilate and yet read on, his gaze fixed to the text. His knuckles were white and he began to grind his teeth.

Quire leaned over and pulled the paperback from the tortured man's death grip. As soon as she did so, he collapsed forward and his forehead slammed into the table. Dazed, he lifted his head for a second before slamming his head again, intentionally this time. Then he did it again with profound force.

Reggie hurried out from the kitchen. "What's going on out here?"

Boomer sat and stared at him as blood ran freely from his broken nose. A gash had opened above his eyes, as well.

The server rushed back into the kitchen. Seconds later he returned with a first aid kit. He limped as fast as he could.

The injured man held out a hand as if to ward Reggie off. "No. Don't. I don't deserve help."

"Let me," Reggie insisted. "You need help."

"Somehow, somewhere along the way, I … uh, I guess I lost my way," Boomer mumbled. "I wasn't always like this. Something went wrong. How did I get it this wrong?"

Reggie placed the first aid kit on the table and opened it, reaching for an antiseptic and gauze. "This is just until we get you to the hospital. You're going to need stitches, maybe some plastic surgery."

Boomer shook his head. "The thing with Carl and Joan, that's all my fault. I know it. I've been bad to her, bad for the kids. No wonder she went to Carl. He's a listener and all I do is talk. I'm so pissed off all the time and I talk and talk and talk and the shit that comes out of my mouth … I'm sorry!"

Boomer's eyes suddenly locked with mine. "Oh, my God," he declared. "I am *such* an asshole!"

With that, he reached into the first aid kit, grabbed the scissors and stabbed himself in the neck three times before Reggie could stop him. Boomer gave us all a bloody grin as he swayed and slipped to the floor.

Reggie grabbed more gauze and yelled for us to call 911. Desperate to save the man who had just threatened his livelihood, the server applied pressure to the wound with gauze. That soaked through. Boomer's cuts were deft and thorough. More blood pumped out in long squirts that soon ebbed to shorter squirts as the man's heart ran out of blood to pump.

Quire left her seat and bent to stay Reggie's hands. "His troubles are over now. It is okay to let him go."

Reggie looked frantic and I was sure he'd go into shock soon. I was in shock myself, too, but less so than when Alek had done much the same thing. Alek was a friend.

The deaths of strangers are much easier, I thought. *Too easy. Maybe so easy that when they are no longer people, just statistics, it's almost okay to let go. It sounds wrong, but we do it all the time. No one cries for dead ancestors.*

I didn't like myself for even wondering about that. I felt like a stranger to myself. Perhaps, with more exposure to the book, something about me was dying, too.

I gave Quire a hard look. "He's gone. Is this supposed to be better?"

She shook her head. "A better man would reform, apologize and go on to make the world a better place. This man saw the enormity of what he was and surrendered."

"What are you saying?" Reggie said. "This poor man kills himself in front of you and that's all you can say? He was a troubled man in pain — "

"You are a good person, Reggie," Quire said. "Your word is a lamp for my feet, a light on my path." Before I could stop her, with bloody hands, she handed him the book.

"Quire! No!" I leaped from my seat but Quire stood between us. She planted her feet. I tried to push past her. It was as if I was trying to push an oak tree aside. I was too late to save the server from the book.

When she offered it to him, he gave it a glance instinctively. The glance turned into a stare. He straightened and, standing over Boomer's corpse, turned page after page. I stared in horrified fascination as a beatific smile spread over his face.

"That's right, Reggie," Quire said gently. "Feel better now?"

"I really do. Thank you for this gift. If you'll excuse me, I should make some phone calls. The authorities will want to come for the body and so forth. I'll get your orders together, to go, if that's all right? I don't imagine you'll want to be here when they arrive."

"Thank you, Reggie," Quire said.

"Cool."

My jaw dropped as Reggie strode back to the kitchen. To my astonishment, no trace of his painful limp remained.

"The thing in our DNA … it's not just a self-destruct code, is it?" I asked.

"Of course not," Quire said. "I am not a monster. The truth will destroy many but it will set the righteous free. Many will be healed. If all goes well with this little apocalypse, that's the gift we have for you."

30

THE PRINTER OF OUR DISCONTENT

I hadn't been home in a long time but there was no point in
going to my parents' house in Williamsburg. I didn't get along
very well with my father. He was often cold and remote. My
mother was usually pleasant but easily upset. I couldn't imagine
sharing all that I'd experienced with either of them. Besides, my
childhood home was the first place the authorities would look for me
and I was sure my parents couldn't keep a secret. It was time to go
talk to my first and best confidant, Summer Mom (also known as
Aunt June). Forty minutes past Williamsburg, we drove to the
outskirts of Newport News.

My parents rented a small house to my mother's sister. Aunt
June taught twelfth grade at Warwick High. My parents were always
busy so I spent my summers with her. When I looked back on my
childhood, it seemed all the good times were in Newport News. I
went to school in Williamsburg but I'd grown up here.

I was eleven years old when, one day into my summer vacation,
I wandered into a martial arts club in an industrial park in Newport
News. There, I met Chuck Kellogg, Krav Maga teacher and former
airman in the USAF. Before he even shook my hand he said, "You
are here for a reason. What is it?"

"My school has a lot of bullies."

"You've been a victim?"

"Yeah, I guess so."

"Then we know your reason. It's good to have a reason. It'll keep you focused when the work gets hard. Training to defend yourself isn't easy."

"Not having the training is harder."

He liked that answer. "You come here to work, you won't be a victim anymore. Agreed?"

We shook on it and only then did he ask my name.

I trained with Chuck every summer until I left for college in Boston. Chuck had worked as an aircraft engine mechanic in the Air Force. It was he who planted the idea in my head that I should join. Chuck became one of my heroes. I wouldn't have traded one summer in Newport News for all my time at home in Williamsburg. I lived for my summer vacations and my time with my summer mother and Chuck set my life's course..

As Quire drove, I ate fish and chips and watched the familiar scenery roll by. "Heaven is a place where nothing ever happens," I told Quire. "It's soothing to be back. Cops killing cops — everything we've seen — seems pretty remote from here. This is nice."

"Wherever there are humans, we find friction and trauma. However, I notice you are getting somewhat used to the carnage." From her tone, it seemed she was neutral about humanity, she could take us or leave us. I thought again about how she described her existence among us. Being in my presence must have been a trial in itself.

"What does someone like you do when you're not here?" I asked. "You seem to know everything."

She shrugged. "Your conscious thoughts often lack clarity."

I let Quire's casual insult slide. "I said Heaven is boring. Is it?"

"Anywhere absent of friction and trauma is a place of joy. I have a high perch from which to observe the details of your world unfold. When your work with the book is done, the whole planet will know an unprecedented level of peace. You can make a heaven on Earth."

"Speaking of friction and Heaven, I knew a girl named Jocelyn once — "

"Yes, the young woman with whom you wished you'd had sex."

"Um … I guess you *do* know everything. I was going to say that she had a vision of Heaven where it was a vast library where you could read any book and — "

"For you, Heaven would be a continuous orgy with a number of Jocelyns, I suppose."

I reddened and said nothing for a few miles.

"I apologize. I have embarrassed you," Quire said. "It is not my usual role to interact with humans. I am to facilitate your mission but not interfere."

"Not interfere? Of course, you're interfering!"

"You are upset — "

"You handed the book to Reggie! What if it had made him crazy and violent like the others?"

"It healed him as I knew it would."

"If you know this shit, why aren't you spreading the scary word by yourself and leaving me the hell alone?"

"Because you represent your kind, Zane. That is our way. If there is to be creative destruction, it must occur because you, a human, chose it. I can only suggest you take a course of action. I am here to guide you and protect the book. I cannot bring harm to a human but I can bring healing. Reggie is a good person. Exposure to his truth could not harm him."

"So he's one of the designated survivors of the apocalypse?"

"Yes, though I do not care for his California salad. Many of the leaves of romaine lettuce were brown and there was not enough crumbled blue cheese for my taste."

"You get to do the healing and I'm the weapon that gets to do all the killing."

Quire shook her head. "The truth only becomes weaponized in the minds and bodies of the guilty."

What flaw there is to exploit comes from within each of us. We do it to ourselves. Oppenheimer told me that when I was in a deep conversation with my subconscious. "Quire?"

"Yes?"

"Whatever the book does to people, it's already done it to me, hasn't it? I'm infected. The Mind Virus is already working on me."

"We behold what we are and we are what we behold," she replied.

"Cryptic and unhelpful."

"The answers will mean more if you figure it out yourself. Before we are done, you will have all your answers."

I had many more questions but I had the distinct impression that I had finally managed to irritate Quire. I wasn't accustomed to talking to a celestial being and the enormity of that fact was just starting to hit me. I'd been a little distracted, surrounded as I'd been with blood and death at every turn. I moved on to my most immediate fear and blurted, "Is the Chicago Police Department trying to find us for questioning?"

"Unquestionably, yes."

"Is Charlotte safe as long as I continue to cooperate?"

"Yes, your friend is safe."

"She was worried about exposing her baby to harsh words in the womb. Given that her husband tried to kill her — "

"If you succeed, the child will be raised in a much safer and better world."

"Then round, round we go," I said. "Seeing as I don't have a choice — let's test more assholes and give this world an enema!"

"But you *do* have a choice, Zane. Nature causes all movement. Deluded by ego, the fool harbors the perception that says, 'I did it!'"

Quire sounded like she was quoting something but I didn't know what.

"I saw the look on your face when you handed the book to Carl at the restaurant," Quire said. "With the musician, you were reluctant to deliver the message."

"I was afraid."

"But you didn't like Carl and the man you called Boomer."

I hadn't told her my nickname for the suicidal cuckold, but somehow Quire knew.

"You didn't like Carl so you allowed yourself to become the messenger. That is fine but I worry."

"Worry? I didn't know you had the capacity to worry, Quire! You talk like a robot."

"After your conversation with Oppenheimer, you are changing. That's fine but you are beginning to enjoy your role."

"I didn't like either of those guys — "

"You misjudged Carl."

"He slept with another man's wife so, no, I didn't think he was a good guy."

"You are not in a position to dictate who is deserving of what punishment or prize."

"Everybody's got an enemy's list, Quire, whether they admit it or not. I'd love to hand the book to a lousy, psychotic financial advisor I had a few years ago — "

"It is not up to you to aim the mortal words for personal gain. You were not given this responsibility to pursue vendettas," Quire scolded.

"You may know everything but you still don't understand how hard it is to be human. There's a lot of friction between people. It leaves scars you can't see. We're made this way. If we're disappointments to you, blame the power behind the book!"

"That friction between people, your fears, is what defines humans most. I wonder what you could become if you had the courage to take away all that has defined you until now. If you are successful, we will find out together. I don't know the future but I do know your chances of success are very tenuous."

"Peace on Earth is all up to me, huh? Makes sense. That was sort of my job description before I fell into this snake pit. That was pretty damn tenuous, too."

I spoke only to give directions to my aunt's house. I couldn't wait to talk to a human.

PART IV

The world is before you and you need not take it
or leave it as it was when you came in.
~ James Baldwin

I keep my ideals, because in spite of everything
I still believe that people are really good at heart.
~ Anne Frank, *The Diary of a Young Girl*

31

JUMP SCARE

I stood on the front step of Aunt June's house. I looked around for a moment. "Every summer I came back here, my best friend was Stephen Chilkors." I pointed to a house two doors down. "That's his place. He went bald, got a work-from-home gig with a tech company and moved back in with his parents to take care of them. I haven't spoken with him in years but Aunt June keeps me up to date."

Quire stared at me, apparently waiting for a punchline.

"It's the eve of the apocalypse and Stephen has no idea what's coming. I wish I were him."

"You carry a heavy responsibility but the cause is just."

"I get it but if I'm the good guy, how come I'm using the reasoning of every bad guy?"

"If you think it is divine justice, will you feel better about it?"

"I guess I'm not quite sure how to break the news to my sweet and gentle Aunt June. What am I supposed to say to Summer Mom, Quire? 'I'm back in town after a long absence with a bunch of bodies in my wake?' Or, 'Hi, June! The human experiment has failed and here comes a reckoning for civilization and, hopefully, a reboot. Oh, by the by, the weapon that will bring about the great cull is the most dangerous book in the world and I happen to be carrying it in my pocket. How about some tea and how's the ulcerative colitis treating you?'"

Before Quire could answer, June opened the door. "I thought I heard a car! Zane! How you doing, baby boy!" She pulled me into a long hug and kissed my cheek, leaving, I was sure, a perfect impression of her lips in bright red. (If Aunt June's lipstick wore off in the slightest she would exclaim, "Oh, my gosh! I'm standing here naked!" Then she'd apply another coat of cherry red.)

Before I could think of how to introduce her, June pushed me aside to hug Quire. I didn't think Quire would be a hugger but she not only accepted the embrace but returned it.

"This is Quire. She's a friend of mine," I said awkwardly.

"A colleague," Quire corrected me.

June giggled. "I'll get you guys a knife to cut the sexual tension. Or have you figured that out, yet?"

"June, it's not like that."

"Well, if true, that's a shame," she said.

We joined in with June's laughter. I thought Quire laughed a little harder than necessary. Still, I have to admit I was beguiled. I'd never heard Quire laugh and she let it come up from the belly, more raucous than I'd expected.

"Have you seen the news?" June asked.

"We heard about it," I said. "That's sort of why I'm here."

"Uh-oh," June said. "I know that look. Serious Zane has shown up. Come in, come in!"

June's house wasn't much more than a small cottage. She hurried ahead of us to mute *CNN*. Stepping into the living room was like stepping back in time. Hardly anything had changed except the couch. Still, I recognized that couch. I remembered the old couch from my last visit home. It looked worn, even a bit ratty.

"Is this — "

"From Chris and May's house, yes. I'm about to retire, believe it or not. I am not about to go out and splurge on a new couch."

"Chris and May are my parents," I told Quire.

"I know."

"The springs were shot on the old one, especially since you spent so much time bouncing on it when you were a kid."

"June — "

"He built pillow forts in this room," she told Quire. "I guess that was a harbinger of things to come."

She must have caught my irritated look because she hurried on. "Anyway, May asked if I'd like their old one. The usual course of these things is old couches go down to the basement before getting kicked to the curb. Free furniture is good."

June was frugal. She never felt comfortable enough to purchase a new sofa at full price. I wondered if I should tell her the apocalypse was well underway so now would be a good time to run up the charges on her credit card.

"Chris and May were very generous., don't you think? I like it, don't you? It's broken in."

"It's fine," I said.

After the apocalypse you'll get what you deserve, I thought. *You'll have more space and much better furniture when you move into the abandoned mansion of some rich asshole who offed himself.*

"How's Colorado Springs?" June asked. "What's doin'? How's the missile business?"

"Still there, for now." My gaze fell on June's small television. It was muted but the pictures and the crawl across the bottom of the screen told me all I needed to know: *The navy is busy in the Persian Gulf, ramping up operations. The Russians are performing unscheduled exercises in the North Atlantic.*

June followed my gaze. "Things are heating up but no one seems completely sure whom to blame. Isn't it terrible about the pope? That sort of thing should go to court — "

"I didn't think the death of the pope would spur these particular demonstrations of force," I said.

"What happened in the Vatican was awful but that's old news now, I suppose," June said.

"The shortening of the human attention span has been progressing in First World nations for the last few decades," Quire said. "What development has replaced the papal suicide?"

June's eyes widened. "You really don't know? The stock market closed after a bunch of traders and regulators threw themselves to their deaths."

"You mean like the stock market crash in 1929?"

"That is a myth," Quire said. "Not that many people committed suicide on Wall Street then — "

"I guess they didn't get the memo and took their cue from the myth," June replied. "A whole bunch of them committed suicide. I saw it happen live. It reminded me of the jumpers on 9/11."

"So they all jumped off the top of the New York Stock Exchange?"

"No, and that's what's got everyone freaked out. As soon as the bell rang this morning, they streamed out of the Exchange and wandered the streets. Wall Street guys were giving away their money, credit cards, watches and rings. Some even wrote checks and took off their clothes to give to the homeless. The news is reporting that they were crying and apologizing to people all over the place. Some people took the cash and thanked them. Most thought they were crazy and ran from them."

"I probably would have backed away from a crying naked man trying to give me money, too," I said.

"When they didn't have anything left to give, they all went quiet and calm. Then they marched into surrounding high rises. They got on to the roof and lined up to go over the side. I'm glad school is out for the summer or I'd be in a classroom right now trying to explain what's happening to a bunch of freaked-out kids. Reporters are calling it mass hysteria or mass hypnosis now. Mass something, anyway. None of the experts they interview say it can be any of that."

"No clues at all?"

"They talked to the traders who were left behind in the mass suicide. They said it was as if the opening bell was a signal. Everybody just got up from their desks at the same time and walked out. It's on every channel but I don't think anyone really knows what's going on."

"I might have an idea." I collapsed on the couch. The small of my back was icy cold where I kept the book. Still, I was sweating heavily. Copies of the book were in circulation. I didn't know how many but at least enough to hit major religious and financial institutions as well as taking a stab at two icons of the justice system.

A fresh breaking news alert flashed on the screen. I reached for the remote and turned up the sound. "We're now getting scattered reports that the prime minister of Russia, Andryusha Fedor, went on a murder spree last night. The massacre occurred in the equivalent of Russia's White House, *Dom pravitelstva Rossiiskoi Federatsii*. Various anonymous sources are saying they heard the sounds of machine gun fire and an explosion in the government building between nine and ten last night, Moscow Standard Time."

The newsreader stared into the camera. "I must emphasize, it's suspected the shooter was Mr. Fedor. We don't know if Russia's president, Vladimir Putin, was in the building at the time. Some government sources say Mr. Putin is in a secure location but we have no confirmation at this time."

In a daze, I spoke to the screen as if the news anchor could hear me. "Are you *trying* to make a cold war go hot? Don't hype the story by implying Putin might be dead. If there's a power vacuum at the top, God knows what happens next."

June looked at me solemnly. "It suddenly feels like anything could happen, doesn't it?"

I felt the sudden urge to hug her again and not let go. When all this was over, I was sure she'd still be standing, ready to be part of Quire's utopia. But first, I had to facilitate a lot more death and chaos.

32

ENSORCELLED

I watched the archive recording of warships on the screen. The media was focused on our destroyers and aircraft carriers. I was more interested in where our submarines might be lurking at that moment. "Things are going to get crazier before we get sane."

"If you are successful," Quire assured me, "sanity will return."

June studied our faces. She probably didn't learn anything from Quire but she must have seen the fear in my eyes. "Zane? You know something. What's going on?"

"It's a long story. I went on stress leave and — "

"Why?"

"Because I was stressed. I get headaches. I've got one right now. At least, I thought I was stressed before. I'm more stressed now."

"Tell me."

"Some very bad things happened in Chicago. Have you talked to my parents recently?"

"I chatted with May last night."

"And she didn't say anything about anyone coming around asking questions about me?"

"No. Zane, you're scaring me. You're in trouble."

I glanced at the screen. "We all are."

Aunt June sat beside me, took the remote from my hand and turned off the television. Taking both of my hands in hers, she gazed into my eyes. "'Fess up."

I told her everything, starting with my meeting with the hawk-faced man. I spared her no detail about the murders and suicides I'd witnessed. June took a few moments to process the enormity of what had occurred and she began to glance at Quire nervously. When I was done telling her about what had happened at the golf course restaurant, she took a deep breath. "And you think it all comes down to a book?"

"I know it does."

"What's in it exactly?"

"All I can remember is a poem on page 124," I admitted. "The man on the train got me to read something but it was just a few gibberish phrases. At least, that's what I thought at the time. When people read from the book, it weaponizes the truth. They do things they wouldn't ordinarily do, act on subconscious impulses — "

"And you don't want to read more in case you end up like the sorcerer's apprentice, brooms and a flood of water everywhere," June observed.

I asked Quire, "Do you know that Mickey Mouse scene?"

"Not really."

"Not *Fantasia*? I thought you knew everything."

"I mainly extrapolate probabilities. I'm familiar with the source material and I did enjoy the poem. It's Goethe." Quire recited:

Gone's for once the old magician
With his countenance forbidding;
I'm now master,
I'm tactician.
All his ghosts must do my bidding.
Know his incantation,
spell and gestures, too.
By my mind's creation

Wonders shall I do.

"SHOW OFF *AND* A NERD!" I said.

June smiled. "She's a catch. Are you sure there's nothing going on between you two because if you're going to face the end of the world as we know it, you shouldn't do it alone. You'd make an adorable couple."

"Ill-timed and impossible," Quire said.

Despite everything, I could not help laughing. I'd been full of so much tension, it had to break somehow and that's how I released it. I wiped tears from my eyes and finally began to relax. "It's funny. I actually *am* a tactician. It's in my job specs! And now I've got the magic incantations. If the Pentagon only knew — "

"Given your expertise, how is this going to end exactly?" June asked.

"Tensions amp up and ramp up but I don't see how this situation can be defined within the strategic responses we've got in the can ready to go. The attacks are pretty random. This isn't a simple territorial dispute over resources. The real estate the government will be trying to defend is in every skull of every citizen on the planet. We don't have a ready response to something on this scale that is this weird. I wonder how much they know or think they know so far."

"Your forces are ill-equipped for such a conflict," Quire said.

I glanced at the dark television screen as if I could still see military forces around the world going through drills and rattling their sabers. "I doubt the United States government is ready to push the nuclear button over the death of a pope. They always have another one in the chamber to take over. However, Russia's response is the big question. The mass suicide at the stock exchange poses so much of a threat to the economy — "

"If this is the end of the world," June said, "I have to break a promise."

"What?"

"I have to tell you something. Chris and May made me promise never to tell you while they were still alive. Since we may all disappear in radioactive vapor, I think it's fair for me to tell you. We should have sat down with you long ago to explain the situation. Once you wait too long, it gets harder and harder to do the right thing."

"The truth will set you free, June," Quire said.

"Wait!" I began. "We are *not* going to ask my aunt to read from the book!"

"I don't need the book to tell you the truth, Zane. When I was young, I made a mistake. I slept with a married man."

I had dim memories of my mother telling me June was dating. That was when I was a teenager. I'd suspected my aunt was a lesbian who chose to keep that part of her life secret from my conservative, judgmental parents.

"It was a brief fling and it was wrong," June continued. "We both knew it. It was a consensual mistake and a consensual breakup. The man went back to his wife and I thought that would be the end of it. Then I was late. The man offered to pay for me to make my little problem go away. I caused him and his wife a lot of trouble by insisting on having that little problem, anyway. That was my last international trip. I made it as far as Montreal and, after a year off work, I came back here with a baby."

"You got pregnant by a married man? I've got a cousin?" I had a hard time imagining anything like this could be a part of June's history. "What happened to the kid?"

"Single motherhood was tough and the man and his wife had money. They raised the baby as their own." She looked at me meaningfully. "He grew up to be a very important person and achieved a high rank in the Air Force at a young age. I'm very proud of him."

I felt dizzy. "Y-you're my mother?"

"And you're my son."

I stared at her in shock. I'd had no idea. She'd slept with her sister's husband. My father. "How did that happen?"

"In the usual way."

"You know what I mean. She was your sister!"

"They were going through a rough time. So was I. In bad moments, sometimes people turn to the wrong people for comfort. Things happen. It's biology. Chris and May needed to talk to each other about their problems. Instead, May shut down. Chris turned to me. We were young and stupid."

"No wonder they were so rigid about me dating. They were convinced I'd ruin my life by getting some girl pregnant. I think I get now why they were such a pain in the ass from the moment I hit puberty."

"I can see that. I'm not proud of it but Chris, May and I have made our peace with it and put it behind us. Their marriage was stronger than one mistake. I want you to know, sleeping with Chris was the mistake. Having you in our lives is a gift. We regretted the affair. I have never regretted you."

Given how cold and stern they could be, I wasn't sure that assertion applied to Chris and May Salvador.

"I'm sorry, Zane. I was alone and your parents had more resources to take care of you."

"Resources? So it came down to money."

"Almost everything comes down to money. I've wanted to tell you many times but, let's face it, I could never have afforded to give you the life you had. Chris is a pharmacist and May has a great job with a pharmaceutical distributor. They could afford to send you to MIT. I couldn't help that way but I always stayed close. Every summer was ours and I have loved you like a son. I am so proud of you."

"That's why you loved it so much when I called you Summer Mom."

Tears slipped down June's cheeks. "I wanted to tell you so many times but there never seemed to be a right time. Chris and May never wanted you to know, at least until they were both dead and gone."

"Good for you, June," Quire said. "You were right. In the end, you didn't need the book to tell the truth. Laudable."

"Funny," I said. "I never thought they could keep a secret. Turns out, they're so good at it, they could work at Cheyenne, too."

I was about to embrace June when two bright pinpoint lasers shone through the window and two shots rang out. The glass in the front bay window shattered as June took two rounds, one to her stomach and one to the upper chest.

She'd been my mother for about two minutes. Then she was shot. June hit her head on the coffee table as she slipped to the floor. Then the blood. So much blood.

33

TO EACH HIS OWN

I threw myself to the floor beside June. She writhed in pain as I put pressure on her wounds and yelled for help.

Quire did not duck and cover or crawl towards us. She strode to me and reached for the book at the small of my back. She yanked it free of my belt and handed it to me. "You believe June is a good person do you not?"

I gaped at her. "What if it does to her what it did to Alek, or Boomer or that cop? She might be the best person I know but she slept with my dad while he was married to her sister. What if she doesn't think she's good enough — "

"She confessed to you. All concerned parties have forgiven each other. She's a good risk."

"I don't know if I believe in that much forgiveness. I mean, I wouldn't forgive her if I were them and — "

"But they did forgive. Neither her condemnation nor her exoneration is your decision."

"Aunt or Summer Mom, I love June. I just don't want to give her the book if it's going to kill her!"

"Zane, if any human can forgive another, don't you think God can manage that small mortal feat?"

From the front and the back of the house, I heard men yelling, "Breaching! Breaching! Breaching!"

With bloody hands, I took the book from Quire as two men burst in the front door. Two more had broken into the house through the back. They all wore white dress shirts and black ties. Clean cut, Caucasian and oh-so-serious, they would have looked like two pairs of door-to-door Mormon missionaries if not for the guns. The muzzles of those guns were pointed at us.

As June struggled for air, the lead assaulter yelled at Quire. "You! On the floor! Show me your hands! Show me your hands!"

Quire raised both hands to show her palms were empty.

"Quire! What page? *What page?*"

"Let the book choose," she said. "The book always chooses its ideal reader."

I had to grab June's jaw roughly to turn her head. "I need you to focus! Look! Look!" I held open the book at a random page. At least, I thought it was random.

The first thing I noticed was that June stopped struggling under me. She relaxed and settled. When I looked up, I realized something else had changed in the room, as well. Our attackers seemed to be frozen in time. None of the gunmen spoke or moved.

"Quire? What's happening? Have you … can you stop time?"

"That would require a gravity bomb that would have ripples across the universe." The way she said it, my ignorance was being mocked by an expert. "I have not changed them," Quire replied. "I have changed your perception."

"How's that?"

"They are still moving, but slower. Your body and brain will not be able to handle this shift in perception for long."

"Impossible."

"Given all you've seen, it's odd that you have not yet redefined impossible for yourself. All manner of species on Earth perceives the world differently than humans. This is just one taste of the possible. When you say 'impossible,' you mean 'outside your experience.' Give June all your attention. Focus!"

Whatever Quire had done to me, I sensed I couldn't stay in this strange hypervigilant state for long. I was exhausted and pain began to blossom and throb behind my eyes.

Zane?

It was June. She smiled up at me. I could hear her thoughts.

I don't feel the pain, anymore.

"Good. Good."

Do you forgive me?

"There's nothing to forgive. All I can say is thank you. Thanks for being you — "

You should read that book, cover to cover. See how it turns out.

I looked up. The gunmen were moving a little now and there was a long, low drone. I was sure they were speaking but their words were so drawn out, their message was indecipherable. "June, there isn't much time — "

"The space of a few breaths," Quire warned, "a few last heartbeats."

I'm okay. I'm all right. Everything is all right now.

June closed her eyes.

"Quire? What's happening?"

"You know."

I checked for a pulse and found none. "But she read the book! She read the book! It didn't make her crazy so why isn't she — "

"Not everyone who is healed lives."

"That's not what healing means."

"She is at peace and, perhaps, off to the next adventure. I have seen many deaths. Hers was a good one."

"The next adventure? You mean she's going to Heaven?"

"When your time comes, you'll find out."

"This is too crazy." Tears slipped down my cheeks. My beloved Summer Mom was dead and I'd brought her killers to her door.

The drone in the background grew louder and was slowly speeding up. The Mormon missionary lookalikes would start making sense soon.

"Why didn't the book save her? It healed Reggie!"

"You are subconsciously equating goodness with long life," Quire replied. "It was June's time. Just because she has passed from this life doesn't mean she was not saved. These are questions beyond human understanding, even beyond mine. This is a realm of the human experience that is opaque to me, private and for each individual. There is order in the universe so I choose to believe your mother is restored."

Suddenly, I was furious. "Restored? What good does that do us? And you don't even *know*?"

"I accept those things I cannot control. To do otherwise is fruitless."

And just like that, my fury dissipated. I was still very tired but the pain in my head was gone. I still didn't understand and Quire's answers frustrated me. They weren't really answers at all. Still, I envied Quire's ethereal calm in the face of death.

"I said, down on the floor!" the lead attacker shouted.

Another home invader tackled Quire and brought her to the ground. I was a little surprised at that. Back at the restaurant when I had tried to get past her, she was immovable.

Her heavily muscled assailant put his knee on her back as he snapped handcuffs on her wrists. She turned her head to look at me. Quire glanced down at the book meaningfully. I knew what she wanted me to do but I wasn't sure it was the right thing.

"Who are you guys?" I asked.

An assaulter leaped over the couch to stand over me. When I looked up, I gazed into the mouth of a very large caliber pistol. "Shut up and assume the position! On your belly!"

"You killed my mother," I said. "Who are you?"

"Shut up!" he repeated. "Shut up and cooperate or I'll blow your head off!"

"Zane!" Quire shouted. "They want to control the book! They only want the message to reach the enemies they choose. That is not the intent of the author!"

I didn't care what 'the author' wanted. Was that the hawk-faced man? Or God? It didn't matter. Neither idea appealed to me.

Quire had been urgent before but until that moment I had never heard a pleading tone in her voice. Even that did not touch my heart. All I knew was that these assholes had killed Aunt June … my Summer Mom … my mother.

I looked down at the book. It was worn and covered in blood and flipped open, its spine broken. The author did not speak to me but they could speak through me. I read aloud to June's killers: "I am tested. Doom rushes upon my enemies."

Furious, I looked in the eyes of each of our captors and thundered, "To each his own death!"

34

GIVETH AND TAKETH

The assaulter who had handcuffed Quire leaped off her back and ran out the front door. The man who had me at gunpoint dropped his weapon and sank to his knees. His sudden weeping turned into wailing.

One of the invaders who had broken through the back door placed his rifle on the floor. With the butt of the weapon on the floor, he went to his knees and tucked the muzzle under his chin. He squeezed his eyes tight. Before his partner could stop him, the man pulled the trigger and with one muffled shot made a mess of June's living room wall.

The remaining assaulter stood slack-jawed beside the body for a moment before looking over at me. "That," he said, "was horrible."

The man beside me wept over June's body and I pushed him away as I got to my feet. The weeping man fell back, then knelt. He bent forward and began to pound his head on the hardwood floor. He did so with more and more fury, once, twice, and then he hauled back and threw himself with every ounce of force he could muster. On the third try, he collapsed into a senseless stupor.

Quire, still handcuffed and face down on the floor, shook her head. "Intracerebral brain bleed. He will not survive the hemorrhage."

If I lived long enough, I promised myself to have an in-depth discussion with Quire about the limits of her perception.

I did not voice that thought aloud but she told me anyway. "I know a lot, but I can't process all the information at once. That would be like you going to a party and trying to hear all the conversations at once."

"All right, you freaks. Enough!" The remaining home invader stood unaffected by the book's curse.

"What agency are you from?" I asked.

"From your friendly neighborhood NYB, the None Ya Business Agency."

"Contractor?" I asked.

The man shook his head. "I stand by my original statement."

He was a heavily muscled guy, the biggest of the four. He held a 9mm Beretta in his right hand but he didn't feel the need to point it at me. Immune to the mind weapon, he looked grim but confident.

"This man is Matthew Henshaw," Quire informed me. "He has close family connections to the security establishment and was recruited out of Princeton to the CIA. He has served in Brazil and in various countries on the African continent. He doesn't know who he's working for or what his employer's objectives are. They sent him after you with minimal information about the book. Despite his outward appearance, he's terrified and confused. Not all his actions have been correct but his heart is pure."

Henshaw stared at Quire for so long, I wondered if she was doing her time dilation thing on him or me. It turned out he was just thinking hard. "You're damn right my heart is pure. For God and country — "

Quire cut him off. "For country, perhaps. I'm trying to save the planet."

The man stepped over Quire to get to me and pointed his weapon at my forehead. "I am sorry about your aunt, Mr. Salvador."

"Update, I only just found out she was my mom."

"Shit, man. I'm sorry. I don't know what to do with that or what to tell you but I do have my orders. Hand over that book."

Slowly, I stooped to pick it up.

"Matthew," Quire said, "You don't mean to do the wrong thing but this is the wrong thing. There are many lives at stake and there is a higher order. Please do not defy it."

An explosion erupted from the street and we heard the whoosh of a sudden fire. Opportunity had offered a hand but that window would close quickly. Despite my weariness, I straightened and tossed the paperback in Henshaw's face as I knocked the pistol aside. The gun went off but the shot went wide.

I brought both fists down on Henshaw's collarbones as hard as I could. At least one clavicle snapped and he buckled a little. I drove my forehead into his nose. The cartilage gave and his nose shifted to one side with a sick crunch that I could feel reverberate through the frontal bone. Before he could recover, I stepped close to drive my right knee into his crotch.

Henshaw was hurt but he was a fighter. He threw his weight against me as he struggled to bring the pistol to bear. I tripped over June's body and fell backward onto the couch.

I clung to Henshaw, keeping him close. I managed to twist the gun out of his grip. We grappled for it for a moment and I screamed in his ear as I pried two of his fingers free and yanked them back with a vicious twist. My assailant yelled in pain as the weapon dropped with a heavy thunk to the wooden floor behind the couch.

With both hands free, he tried to clutch at my throat. In one savage clap, I brought both my hands down hard on his ears. My palms burst his eardrums but it was the strike of the heels of my hands at the jaw joints that made his eyes roll up as he lost consciousness.

Panting hard, I struggled to roll Henshaw's weight off me.

That would have been the end of it except the other man who had knocked himself out stirred and had crawled to his feet.

He picked up the book and his big pistol was back in his hand. His forehead was bleeding and he looked dazed.

Sitting on the couch and still gasping for air, I was in no position to deal with a fresh attack. Wiping the sweat from my eyes, I said, "I thought you were supposed to be dying of a brain bleed."

The man swayed on his feet and looked from Quire to me. "I see how it is now. I don't deserve to die like this. I don't deserve to die in my damned sleep. Stay where you are or I'll shoot you. And I am sorry about your mother. I did that. It was me. Me and my buddy, we shot her right through her front window. That was wrong. I've done a lot of wrong. I'm sorry. I gotta take this with me."

Clutching the book to his chest, he wandered toward the front door and headed for the street.

35

JUSTICE SERVED SWEET AND SOUR

"Stop him!" Quire pleaded.

I was still trying to catch my breath. "He ... said he'd shoot me ... if I didn't stay put."

Quire flipped on her back and rolled to her feet with her hands still cuffed behind her back. It was a maneuver I doubted I could replicate. She made it look easy.

"Get the book, Zane! He won't shoot you and he won't make it far. Trust me." With that, she brought her hands forward. She had not slipped the handcuffs or picked the lock. She'd broken the titanium chain.

I gawped at her a moment before staggering out after the fleeing man. The front door was still wide open and the early afternoon sun baked the street. My jaw dropped as I stared at the carnage before me. As the man with the book and the mortal brain bleed staggered away, I saw the source of the explosion that had distracted Henshaw.

The first man to run out of the house screaming had been on a suicide mission. At a glance, I guessed what he had done: torn his shirt and made a fuse of the cloth for his SUV's gas tank. He must have lit the fuse and jumped into the vehicle to await his fate. I could see his blackened body amid the flames.

The man with the book rushed to the SUV and pulled on the doors. Apparently, all were locked. The mercenary who had burnt himself alive had been committed to receiving no rescue.

The man with the book staggered on. All my energy was gone. The air felt still, stale and tropical and I got little respite as I tried to suck more oxygen into my lungs. Still out of breath from the fight, I doubted I could catch him. My doubt didn't matter because the man who killed June didn't get far. Blue flames burst at his feet and encircled his legs and torso. He had claimed the book and now the flames took him. He dropped the smoking paperback and, with a fresh burst of speed, broke into an awkward run as he began to scream.

Quire appeared beside me in the doorway. "I'd hoped to spare him that fate."

The man kept screaming as he burned. Neighbors emerged from their homes, staring in horror. The government agent finally seemed to notice he'd lost the book and turned around. He began to stagger in a ragged zigzag pattern. His mind was gone. All that remained was pain.

"Is this what he meant by getting the death he deserved?" I asked.

"Our ends would have been equally served if he'd succumbed in his sleep."

"For his sins, he chose that?"

"Not for his sins," Quire said. "For his guilt. Humans justify their actions. They tell themselves they are good or at least no worse than the rest. Deep down, they know the truth they deny."

"Does this death earn him redemption?"

"No, only a worse death. He's punishing himself. It is his choice."

I looked down at Quire's wrists, each with a bracelet of carbon steel. "You could have stopped this. Henshaw almost killed me."

"I am not the messenger," she said. "It's not up to me to interfere with your path. I'm here to protect the book. If it gets too far from me, the bearer ignites. As you can see, death by fire is one of the most unpleasant expirations."

Expirations, I mused. *What an odd, aseptic choice of words. June's killer had reached his expiration date, his best before date ... and I felt no pity for him. If he could kill June as he had, I agreed with him: He did need to suffer and die.*

Several neighbors were screaming. Some yelled for him to stop, drop and roll. Most just screamed. As the man dropped dead to the pavement, everyone suddenly went quiet out of respect for the impromptu cremation service.

Reading my thoughts, Quire assured me, "Many people need to die. You do accept that now, don't you?"

"I didn't think I would but I'm beginning to understand now. I get it. June thought every kid she taught was worth fighting for but ... no, I guess not."

Quire nodded and patted me on the shoulder. "Thank you, Zane."

She strode out to retrieve the book. I turned back to the living room to retrieve handcuffs from the man who'd blown his head off. I pulled them from his belt and slapped the cuffs on Matthew Henshaw.

The mercenary was still out of it but slowly rousing. He'd hurt a while, but he'd live. Despite appearances, he was one of the designated survivors of the coming apocalypse.

"I guess you can never tell who's got a heart of gold just by looking," I said.

That chore done, I returned to my mother's side to say goodbye. "I'm sorry I found out too late," I told her, "but besides that one detail, I wouldn't change a thing. I always thought of you as more of a mom than an aunt, anyway. You know that. Thanks for all those great summers."

Henshaw came around and winced as he rolled on his back. With his hands pinned behind his back, his broken bones must have been agony. His nose bled profusely and his eyes were already turning black. As he tried to suck air, it was apparent his nasal passages had become narrow and wet paths, difficult to thread. "Is it worth it, Salvador?"

"The book, you mean?"

"The blood," he said.

I considered all the death I'd seen. The man in the corner covered in blood had two more holes in his head than when he'd woken up that morning: an entry wound and a gory exit wound.

"I didn't plan this, Mr. Henshaw. I'm not the author of this destruction. I'm on a roller coaster and there's no way off until the ride is over."

Despite the damage I'd done to his eardrums, he could hear me fine. "Not what I asked."

"That dead woman on the floor? She was a good person. I'm having a hard time seeing it right now but apparently you're basically a good person, too. As for your crew, I'm going to trust the book and say everybody else got their just desserts. This feels righteous."

"No mercy in your book, huh?"

"More mercy than your guys showed my mom."

36

THE TIME FOR ALL GOOD MEN

S tephen Chilkors, my best friend in Newport News, waited in front of the house. Slouched against Quire's Stingray, he looked troubled. When I walked up to him with blood on my shirt and looking haggard, he looked even more concerned. Before I could say anything Stephen asked if June was okay. I shook my head and more tears slipped down my cheeks.

He hugged me hard. He gave me a minute, then stepped back to hold me by the shoulders. "I saw those guys roll up. I was working on my computer when I looked out the window. I saw two of them with rifles. One of them was the guy who set his truck on fire and jumped in. I tried to call the police, Zane. I swear I did. My cell didn't work. I'm so sorry. Mom and Dad haven't been well and we've been economizing. I got rid of the television and the landline. I couldn't call the cops and — "

"It's cool, Steve. You tried. It's a blackout."

"I don't understand what's going on."

I looked around. Adults were covering young eyes and shooing kids back indoors, away from the scene from hell. I felt invisible. All they could do was stare at the remains of the burnt men. "The guys who attacked June's house shut down the local cell phone network," I muttered absently.

"They can do that? Just shut down phone service?"

I gave him a grim smile. He had no idea what they could do. I knew because, until recently, I was one of the people who could order that sort of tactic. I expected Stephen to ask more questions. He didn't ask the questions I would have asked. Instead, he asked how he could help.

Quire appeared at my elbow holding the book. There was blood on the cover. It was beaten up and dirty but it hadn't burned up.

"Anything you need, Zane, you know that. Just tell me what I can do for you."

"Do you have a vehicle we could borrow?" Quire asked.

Stephen looked at her for a beat.

"She's with me," I said.

"Then take these." He handed me his car keys and pointed to an old green Toyota Corolla in his driveway. "The tank's only half full and the air conditioning feels like the hot breath of a panting dog but it'll get you somewhere far from here. That would be good. The cops are going to show up eventually."

"You don't need to know more?" I asked.

"They killed June, right?"

"They did."

"Then screw them and no, I don't need to know more than that. I've lived two doors down from your aunt all my life."

I hugged him briefly and started for the car. "Give us as much time as you can. Report your car stolen tomorrow so you keep clear of any blowback. It shouldn't get ugly but if it does, tell them we headed south."

"Got it. Go."

Quire hung back and opened the book to show something to Stephen.

From our previous conversation, I knew she could not bring harm to a human, at least not personally or on purpose. Still, I panicked at the thought of my childhood friend being exposed to the raw powers of the book. Watching Stephen reading from it made me feel as if we were little children with sticky fingers playing with a loaded pistol. "Quire! What are you doing?"

As soon as the words were out of my mouth, I regretted them. My instinct to protect my friend revealed that deep down and despite everything, I still didn't trust Quire to do the right thing. It didn't matter in the end. I was too late. Stephen straightened his spine and shot me a beatific smile. He bowed to Quire and thanked her profusely before walking back toward his house. As he passed me in the street, I saw the light in his eyes. He was different in a way I couldn't quite pinpoint. "You okay, Steve?"

"Never better. I'm still sorry about June. I'm even sad for the burned men — "

"But?"

"There's a feeling in my chest, as if I'm full of helium."

"A body full of helium would make you talk funny before it killed you."

Walking backward, he kept beaming that big smile at me. "I feel so light, it's like I might float up into the sky if I don't concentrate on staying down here. Your friend told me to memorize this one strange word and go tell my mom and dad. I'm going to go do that now. This is going to be great!" Before I could say more, he turned and bounded into his house.

Quire grabbed my elbow and hurried me to our new getaway car. We were down the street and away as wailing sirens rose and faded into the distance.

3 7

THE WEAKNESSES WE ARE HEIR TO

Once we were well on our way, I crawled into the back seat to lie down. Partly, I wanted to stay out of sight. Mostly, relentless exhaustion required that I lie down. Quire pulled the car onto the US-17, heading north as I wept quietly for June.

Mother or aunt, the label didn't matter now. I'd always looked upon her as a friend and I was grateful to have known her. How many sons honestly look upon their parents as friends? I certainly didn't feel the same way toward Chris and May Salvador.

"Do you have injuries that need to be addressed?" Quire asked.

"Mostly just psychological wounds now, I think. My mother — May, I mean, not June — told me that she named me after Zane Grey, an author. His westerns were the only books my grandfather ever read. Dad said I was lucky I didn't get stuck with the name Pearl. Pearl Zane Grey was the author's full name."

"Do you want to go to your parents now, to speak with them?"

A bitter laugh erupted from me as I sat up. "Given that the world is falling apart, I don't think I have time to unpack all the lies with them. No time for soap opera."

Despite the heat of the day, my back felt ice cold again. I shivered as I pulled the book from the small of my back and tossed it on the floor of the car.

Quire caught my eyes in the rearview mirror. "Are you sure you are not injured?"

"Nothing I can't walk off. It's shock. I left Cheyenne to get away from war and I've run smack into it at home. When I was a little kid, I worried about getting sick but I always assumed I'd never go crazy. Not so sure now."

"You are not mentally ill, at least no more so than the average human being."

"Is that how you see us? Messed up mentally?"

"Not all of you, but enough of you are ignorant, intolerant, racist or foolish to be dangerous."

"I don't think those things qualify as mental illnesses per se."

"Aren't they?"

I didn't know what to say to that.

"You are not mentally ill," she assured me again. "Aphonenia is the tendency to see patterns where there are none. I can assure you, there is reason amid the patterns you see. You're here to find an epiphany amid the norms to which you have become accustomed."

"Great," I muttered listlessly and stared out the window. My back was still uncomfortably cold and I felt the urge to urinate. I decided to hold it rather than pull over. The more miles between me and the horrors at June's house, the better. The big sign for the Yorktown Battlefield Colonial National Historical Park told me we hadn't gone nearly far enough from the crime scene.

"June took me here a couple of times," I told Quire. "She said whoever named the park must have been paid by the letter. I wonder if it will ever feel right to call her mom. And calling May my mother …? That's gonna be weird now."

Quire spoke in a tone I hadn't heard from her until that moment. She spoke softly, gently hinting at the truth. "That may not be a problem you will have to face, Zane."

Of course, I thought. *When the words reach Chris and May Salvador, maybe they'll kill each other with the hatchet and hammer that hang on the wall in the garage.*

The powers of the book had failed to bring June back from the brink of death. However, according to my guide, she had not been judged harshly. The way Quire spoke, I suspected my family would not be so lucky.

"Whatever happens, it is just," Quire assured me. "There's a code hidden within each of you. You decide your fate. It's just a question of activating the program hidden in your software. You judge yourselves. Think of the book as a mirror. When you see yourself as you really are, you either forgive yourself — "

"Or get sentenced to death by embarrassment."

"When the time comes, the world will need you to act on what you know, Zane. Can you do it?"

"I think so. After dealing with Henshaw's crew, the rest of us would be better off without those kinds of people dragging us down."

"But?"

I shrugged. "It's one thing to fantasize about executing bad people. It's another to actually do it. I don't really believe in evil. I believe some people have bad brains that are ruled by fear."

"That is correct. The people the book will eliminate all have enlarged amygdalae. They are easily triggered into feelings of fear, disgust and anger."

"If they've got bad biology, isn't it evil to kill them for thoughts that are beyond their control — "

"Actions are under their control," Quire argued. "To use the book as you must will take great courage. As Shakespeare wrote, 'The evil that men do lives after them. The good is oft interred with their bones.' With this reset, the good you do with the book will echo through generations to come. You're going to give humanity a fresh start. You must rid yourselves of the worst in order to preserve the best."

38

DEATH BENEFITS

"I guess the book makes us do our worst to ourselves. We let the weakness in, same as it's always been." Passing by the park, a new thought occurred to me. "The Siege of Yorktown was like that."

"Oh? Please explain."

"I grew up around here. I've heard the story many times, in school and as part of my military studies. The siege lasted three weeks. Imagine constant bombardment, day and night. The cannons didn't rest and neither did the soldiers. In the end, 6,000 British troops surrendered to the Americans and the French."

"Human warfare is barbaric. It lacks elegance."

"One of the reasons the British couldn't mount a defense was malaria. The Virginians grew up around the marshlands and had some built-in resistance to the disease. The French hadn't been here long enough for the symptoms to take hold. Cornwallis said he couldn't fight us off because half of his fighting force was debilitated with malaria. Hard to say, though. He was a bit of a whiner. When the time came, he wouldn't even surrender personally. He went to bed and called in sick. That was probably about ducking the humiliation. The officer who was sent to surrender the sword got dicked around, too. He presented the sword to the French commander who then told him to give it to Washington. Washington told him to surrender to the guy next to him. Classic petty ball-busting shit."

"Are you likening the effects of the mortal words to a disease?" Quire asked.

"Oppenheimer told me the book was going to get rid of the assholes. Assholery is the disease that keeps us from fighting off the book's negative effects. Some people say this is the best time to be alive. I'm not so sure. Maybe it wasn't better for a lot of people in the past but it could be a whole hell of a lot better now. I thought we'd all be a lot better by now. We've got a new disease now: the disease of bad information. The internet has allowed us to spread the poison around, to infect each other easier. Why have we got to be so goddamn mean to each other?"

"That is the human condition and its origin springs from many variables. Peaceful coexistence and welcoming of the other is not prevalent in your history, Zane. That is what frightens me most about your kind. Only eight percent of Earth's recorded history passed in peace. War has become such a static state in this century your peacetime is largely indistinguishable from war. The book arrives at a critical time."

"And here you are, coming to save us from ourselves. Which horseman of the apocalypse are you, Quire?"

"I'm here to help you save yourselves from your worst impulses. And I'm not one of the four horsemen from Revelation. You are. You're the one on the red horse carrying a sword, the one with the power to make men slay each other."

I picked up the book and glanced at the cover. The odd-looking figure silhouetted in fire seemed to be mocking me. I hefted it. It felt too light to make much of a difference in the world. Somehow, it seemed as if it should be heavier.

"It's not exactly a couple of tablets brought down from a mountain destined to change the world, is it?" Quire observed.

"I don't like it when you read my mind," I said.

"You can relax. It's not as if I'm rummaging around in your skull. I just get snatches of your thoughts, here and there." She blessed me with a rare smile. "I find your thought process is very chaotic. I don't know how you get through a day."

I pointed at my skull. "It's dark in there."

"That's a joke, correct?"

"Never mind. I'm not up to teaching you the way of humans. Why a book, Quire?"

"Please expand on your query."

"Most people don't even read books anymore, do they? There are probably more armpit fetishists and furries than there are people who read more than one book a year. You'd get more eyeballs making a meme for the net. Put your curses and magic healing spells under a video of kittens wrestling with yarn and the whole country will grind to a halt tomorrow. That would really weaponize this thing." I tossed the paperback on the seat and stared out the window.

"The book is the beginning. So far, this is merely a test run."

"Oh? Got big plans for a graphic novel, do you? You've got strong imagery in people burning alive but I'm not sure it's going to get picked up by Marvel or DC."

I was past my fear and the grief. I was angry. "How do you imagine you're going to purge the world of all the bastards? Make it into a movie? It would be great to have Dwayne Johnson or Jason Momoa play the role of the messenger, but let's face it, I don't fill out the uniform that way. Tom Hanks is a nice guy. Surely, he'll be available after the apocalypse but I don't know how much of Hollywood will be left once we make everybody read the book. This is crazy. If this magical mystery tour is going to make a real impact, we're going to have to rent a big bus and get me to do readings from a big stage."

I knew I was blathering, maybe on the edge of hysteria. Still, I continued, speaking fast, the words seeming to spill out ahead of any rational thought. "This is a stupid plan! To get people to show up to a book reading, we're going to have to have killer opening acts. You're going to have to reunite the Beatles, the living and the dead! Bring Freddie Mercury, Prince and George Michael back from the dead while you're at it and — "

183

"Zane — "

"To get everybody to pay attention, I'll have to deliver the divine wrath of God at the halftime show of the Super Bowl. And they'll have to be playing football in the middle of a NASCAR race and — "

"Zane!"

"*What?*"

"This is a trial run. The attacks in other countries were a demonstration."

"A demonstration to whom?"

"It's all been for you. All of it, for you."

I stared at Quire in the rearview mirror as we crossed the bridge over the York River. "All this death is for my benefit? That's not what death benefit means, Quire."

"You had to be prepared. We need you to understand the why of what you need to do. We had to show you the need of what is to come. Your species is destroying itself. Approximately a third of your populace experiences fear and converts that emotion to anger and disgust. Another third simply experiences naked fear and, paralyzed in helplessness, remains silent. The remaining third are somewhat open to reason. Poor odds for long-term survival of your species, wouldn't you agree?"

"Seems a bit too reductionist," I said. "We've made it this far."

"I can break it down further to a 50/50 analysis, if you prefer. Of those who participate in public discourse, roughly half of you is against the other half. Those who opt out are merely hoping to be ignored and left alone, as if positive outcomes occur without positive action."

"That's a pretty grim obituary for the human race."

"What is about to happen is not genocide. You're going to save the world."

"I'm not Superman, Quire."

"No, but you are in a unique position to be the messenger. You were correct that there aren't enough readers of books anymore. However — "

I swallowed hard. I'd finally received my epiphany. "But every-body's got a cell phone."

"If we are to go forward, I need you to be sure of your decision."

"Head west," I said. "I'm turning to page 124 again."

"I need your answer, Zane."

"And I need to sleep on it." I couldn't wait to lapse into a deep dreamless sleep where nothing could reach me.

PART V

Precisely at the point when you begin to develop a conscience
you must find yourself at war with your society.
~ James Baldwin

What is done cannot be undone, but one can prevent it happening
again. ~ Anne Frank, *The Diary of a Young Girl*

39

BAD ODDS AT BRIARGATE

The trip back to Colorado took twenty-seven hours of straight driving. I slept through most of it, waking a few times when we stopped for the three Fs: food, fuel and fecal evacuation. I asked Quire if she needed to sleep or eat. She replied that such needs were "unnecessary." I got the feeling she meant my biological needs were beneath her.

When we got back to Colorado Springs I directed Quire to my apartment in Briargate. I was well-rested but I had to shower and shave. That done, I put on my uniform. It was odd to think this was the last time I would wear it. It always struck me a little funny that the uniform in Cheyenne is the Airman Battle Uniform rather than the ultramarine blue. The ABU is very similar to camo but I work in an office. The most appropriate battle dress for me would be a calculator.

Last times spur memories of first times. I took great pride in my uniform later on but all I remembered about my first time in uniform was a sergeant screaming instructions at me on how to stand at attention and wear it right.

As I emerged from the bathroom, I found Quire moving slowly around my small apartment. She scanned the spines of my books

189

and examined the photographs on my shelves as if it were an exotic museum exhibit. When she turned to find me in full uniform, my guide to the Word Apocalypse seemed uneasy.

"I'm ready," I said. "Drive me to the demarcation point. No one can just drive in to the complex. There's a bus. If there's a problem at the first checkpoint, all that you've done to prepare me will have been for nothing. June … my mother's death will be for nothing."

"It is likely there will be a problem getting in," Quire said. "The investigation of the battle at June's house points to your involvement. Civilian authorities have alerted your superiors and the guards will try to escort you to your superiors. They will not allow you to get to your command center without resistance."

I began to sweat.

"Not all of us have quasi-omniscience, Quire. Now I wish I didn't know to expect trouble. Are you sure that's how it will unfold?"

"Highly likely, yes. Better for you to be prepared."

"Then what do I do? If anyone in the complex gets a hint that there's trouble at the first gate, they'll go into full shutdown. That little book is a pocketful of miracles, curses and God's wrath but it just works on minds. Unless it's got powers you haven't even hinted at yet, I don't think it's going to let me ghost my way through a twenty-five ton blast door. The complex is built to withstand a thirty-megaton hit. How's little ole me going to breeze through without clearance?"

"Perhaps you could read the guards a story."

"But it doesn't work the same on everyone. These are strong-minded people committed to their nation's security. They haven't been shown the big picture. The book didn't work on Henshaw, remember? He damn near killed me."

"It will work on most."

"It only takes one to shoot me in the face. You said yourself that the book is not for everyone. What if I give them the snow lullaby and put them to sleep?"

"That doesn't work unless they're exhausted or want to sleep already."

"Shit. That one's more like straight hypnosis, huh?"

"I have posited multiple scenarios and potentialities. Go in expecting resistance. That is most realistic."

"Nice to know there are limits and loopholes. Navigating the book's rules feels like walking through a minefield."

"It's fairly straightforward from my point of view. You have free will to do as you please. The book raises awareness of the impact of your actions. Your words and deeds make the sum of what you have become. If the guards at the checkpoint fall when their truth is exposed, it is just."

"If they just take themselves out, maybe, but I've seen suicidal people turn to murder first. Why kill others — "

"Rage at others is inextricably tied with rage at the self. That same rage drains empathy and makes humans blind to consequence."

"I'll try to keep the carnage to a minimum but the necessary dead are inevitable. I don't know if I can live with that."

Quire looked interested. "The necessary dead? You are obsessed with that phrase."

"It's a term we use. Collateral damage is the death of innocent people when we're targeting bad ones. Acceptable loss is the percentage of collateral damage we decide we can take to fulfill mission objectives. When innocent people are sacrificed, we call them the necessary dead. Should have called the book that: *The Necessary Dead*. Has a ring to it."

"You are very concerned," Quire said. "Is there something else you wish to clarify?"

"I'm just thinking of the guys on the gates. It's a terrible thing to do to them."

"Only if they are among the chosen to die and they choose their fate — "

"I know! I know! Thing is, I don't think those guys are assholes. Strident and rigid sometimes, but I've been that, too. I don't agree with everybody's politics but I don't have to — "

"The curses are unleashed from within. The power goes deeper than transient opinions about politics."

191

"I get that, but I've been assigned to Cheyenne for five years! I know some of them, at least a little. It feels different when the necessary dead have names you know."

"As you said, if you don't do what's necessary now, all that has come before will have been for nothing."

"That's the sunk cost fallacy. That same reasoning has kept us spending more blood and treasure because we've already spent a lot of blood and treasure. If war was Vegas, all the generals and politicians are broke and just keep rolling the dice on the taxpayer's dime."

"Will you commit to this course of action or not?" Quire demanded.

"It depends. Does your plan have any hope of success?"

"If it goes awry, I am prepared to help you complete your task."

"How?"

"If you meet resistance at the first gate, I can help."

"I thought you operated under the Prime Directive."

She gave me a blank stare and it was my turn to sigh. "You don't know *Star Trek?*"

"The database of human experience is a rich tapestry. Not all of it interests me equally."

"Well, that sounds like disrespect and blaspheming to a *Trek* fan. After this is over, look it up. It's about humanity exploring the galaxy, learning lessons and making love to aliens."

Quire startled me by bursting out laughing. "According to my studies, learning lessons and making love to aliens is *highly* unlikely. In your films, humans are intrigued when they encounter the unfamiliar. In reality, most would either run away screaming or try to kill anything alien to them. You barely tolerate each other when you are different colors."

"You said you don't interfere in human affairs."

"Once you've decided on the prescribed course, I can help facilitate that action."

"So you aren't just an observer, after all," I said.

"Sacrifices for the greater good must sometimes be made. In this case, the greater good is avoiding the complete extinction of your species."

"That's the math of it."

"That is the script we must follow to the end."

"They're going to kill the messenger, you know. I'm pretty sure. Do your powers of prognostication agree?"

"Yes."

"Great, it's a suicide mission. What happens afterward?"

"After what?"

"What's my heavenly reward? I had a friend who was hoping Heaven would be an eternal library with all the answers to life's questions and, presumably, comfortable seating. Is that it for me? Is it hot hookers and a bottomless bag of cocaine? Do I get to bask in the eternal glow of the presence of the divine, kind of just marinating in it? I want to know if this is all going to be worth it. I want to matter. If I'm going to do this, it better damn sure mean something."

"You are becoming agitated again."

"How about a harp? Do I get a harp and a one-on-one with the big guy? A coupon for a chocolate shake at McDonald's? Will the mysteries of the universe be revealed? Do I at least get an after-action debrief to find out what went right and what went wrong?"

She brightened. "Yes, that is a good idea. I believe I can give you a debriefing. That would be kind. I can promise you a reward."

I stared at her for a moment. I found it disconcerting to surprise her. Apparently, my death and whatever meaning it might have to me personally was of little or no consequence to the universe. The math on that checked out, actually. Most of the universe was pretty cold, incompatible with human life and disinterested in our desires.

"Let's do this thing before I change my mind."

40

AQ

We took my Ford Bronco to the complex. I wanted to buy a Subaru but when I came to Cheyenne it was made clear to me that General Pitmore preferred staff who bought American-made. To my knowledge, he never checked what we drove to work but somehow rumors go around and around until they become settled law. It was said the general also liked officers whose families were military or former military. Members of the Masons also got preferential treatment. I couldn't do anything about the fact that my father was a pharmacist and I wasn't interested in Freemasonry so I bought a Bronco.

My ears popped as we climbed the long curving road up to the first checkpoint. I wondered if I'd be in this position if I'd been truer to myself and a little more defiant. Would I be God's chosen messenger to wipe out a billion or three if I'd bought the Subaru Forester?

"Zane, whatever happens, will happen. Commit to the script," Quire told me.

I didn't want to talk anymore. I wanted to be somewhere else, anywhere else. I wondered where Jocelyn was and what she was doing now. I had seen her around campus but we had not said more than hello since I shut my door in her face.

The last time I spotted Jocelyn, she was walking out of the library with some guy, hand in hand. They looked happy. I wished I had it in me to be glad for her but all I could think was how I wished I was her lover. I'd had to report for duty at Fort Bragg and missed the graduation ceremonies so I never had a chance to say a proper goodbye. I never even gave her a proper apology.

Quire lay down in the back seat as I parked the Bronco in the parking lot. The main entrance was nowhere near the first check-point but it was the beginning of a shift. Other staffers were also parking their cars. I paused to look in the rearview mirror. She was behind me but I couldn't see her. "Goodbye, Quire."

"Let go of your fears. I'll see you again soon."

"On the other side?"

She did not reply to that. Instead, she asked in a pleading tone, "You *will* send the message, won't you, Zane?"

"Oppenheimer worked out his math and fathered the bomb. I feel like I'm about to do something like that, but much worse. Still, I can't deny the math. Kill billions of bad people, save the rest. I get it."

"Free the planet of the subset of people that are bringing the species down," Quire said. If she'd meant to be encouraging or comforting, she missed the target.

I felt like I should say something more but I didn't know what. It was as if I was standing at the edge of a hole that was about to become a mass grave. What would the world say if I put it to them: If you could rid the world of all the assholes that make life worse, would you?

I knew the quick and easy answer was: No, because who gets to decide?

That variable was at the crux of this elegant solution. The assholes would suddenly get enough clarity to decide for themselves whether they lived or died. It was an elegant, egalitarian equation that absolved me of responsibility, but only somewhat. What was the acceptable percentage of collateral damage when the action was on such an enormous scale? How many necessary dead was a small enough number?

"Zane? Are you going?"

"Yes," I said. "I was just thinking."

"You have doubts."

"Of course, I do. I've always been proud of my Intelligence Quotient. I was so excited about my IQ, I couldn't wait to join Mensa. Now I'm wondering what my AQ is."

"AQ? Ah, Asshole Quotient."

"You would think intelligence and assholery are mutually exclusive but they are not. I'd give anything to be a sweet-natured idiot right about now."

"Go save the planet, Zane. And leave your keys."

"You want to listen to the radio?"

"When the plan goes awry, I'll need the keys."

"Sure. Sure." I climbed out of the Bronco and paused in the doorway.

"Can you tell me if Charlotte is still okay? Has she had the baby? Is she safe?"

"She was never in danger from us. She's in danger from you."

"Me?"

"Humans threaten humans. I'm here to save you from yourselves."

"Bye, Quire."

"I'll see you again."

"But will I see you?" I slammed the door and headed toward the checkpoint. The book was in my briefcase. It suddenly felt very heavy. It wasn't the weight of the case that slowed me down. It was the weight of the mission.

41

GATEWAY

Five guards manned the first checkpoint. One hung back behind the bus on the other side of the road, watching the blind side. I knew most of the guards on sight but we were never really friendly or familiar. The detail on the gate had an interesting ethos. They seemed easygoing with each other but made a show of taking their jobs very seriously when it came to checking us in.

Despite their youth — all the guards were under thirty — they acted like strict parents, as if everyone who passed their gate was a drunk teenager out past curfew. Dealing with security and putting up with General Pitmore were possibly the only two elements of my job I did not enjoy at Cheyenne. Being on the inside had, until that moment, made me feel special, in on defense secrets very few were allowed to know.

All staff entering the facility had to be wanded, searched and checked for contraband. The security protocol reminded me of airport security anywhere, except the guards were better armed and even more surly. They had a right to be. On the far side of security lay the machines that were the keys to the ignition of nuclear war.

The day bus driver was usually the same guy, an old sergeant named Ed who looked very much like the actor, Ed Harris. He knew me by name and was the friendliest of the bunch. Still, every day he would check my badge as I boarded the bus, his eyes shifting from the photo to my face. He'd wish me a good morning and I'd say, "Still not a plant person from *Invasion of the Bodysnatchers*, Ed."

"As far as we know," Ed would always reply.

The last day of my life was not routine. I took my time in the parking lot, making sure I was the last to arrive. Unlike TSA security, they would not rush me through because I was late. Security was more important than the schedule. If I was really late, the bus would leave without me. My strategy was to make sure the staff was on the bus and out of harm's way if things got as ugly as Quire predicted.

It got ugly quickly. As soon as one of the guards spotted me walking in from the parking lot, I saw him pick up the phone in the guard shack. The investigators of the massacre in Newport News must have reached out. The guards had been waiting for me to show up. It suddenly occurred to me that I should have approached the checkpoint with the book in hand. I didn't fancy the idea of being in handcuffs when someone glanced in the book and decided a murder-suicide spree was the order of the day.

I held up the badge on my lanyard. "Lt. Colonel Zane Salvador, SCIS." I'd been with Cheyenne's Survivable Communications Integration System since I'd been assigned. I thought I'd hit the right note, somewhere between confident and nonchalant but I already knew by the look on the guard's face that I wasn't going to be able to bluff and breeze my way through.

The guard on the phone snapped his fingers and all eyes were on me. He leaned out of the doorway and called out, "Lt. Colonel Salvador! General Pitmore would like you to report to his office immediately. I will accompany you, sir. No bus for you today. We'll take you in a Jeep, sir."

Other staff who had been going through the checkpoint and boarding the bus looked back at me. Some looked surprised to see me. Some brows furrowed. The implication was clear. Nobody was giving me a ride into the complex because I needed a lift and help to find the general's office. I was going to arrive at his desk under arrest.

I wondered how much they knew or thought they knew. It was classic Pitmore to have the guard yell to me in front of everyone. I felt like a naughty boy getting called down to the principal's office. Civilians and the military are far apart on most things but that Venn diagram overlaps mightily in one commonality: the pettiness of office politics.

The general and I never warmed to each other. A colonel trying to help my career had tipped me off that Pitmore thought I was too cautious, too much of a dove for the job. He only wanted hawks on his watch. Ironic, considering what I was about to do.

"I'll take your case for you, sir." The guard said it at about the same time as he pulled it from my grasp.

Quire had said, 'When the plan goes awry,' not if. I wondered then: Was she better at the mathematics of managing probabilities than I was? Was she an angel or a demon?

"There's a weapon in the case," I said.

The guard paused a moment. "Why's that, sir?"

"It's not locked."

Many of my colleagues sat on the bus. They watched me through the windows, some furtively, a few with open stares.

The catches popped with a couple of loud clicks and the guard peered into the case. Given that civilian authorities wanted me for questioning in connection with mass murder, it was a thoughtless move. I could have rigged a grenade to explode when he inspected the case. However, he'd seen me come in and out of the complex many times. Vigilance drops as familiarity increases. "It's just a paperback," he said.

"The weapon is concealed in the book." The other guards looked to me, suddenly tense. They did not shoulder their rifles but they shifted in place, planting their feet, ready for action. I put both of my hands out to the sides to show they were empty.

The guard quirked an eyebrow at me as he put the case on the ground. As he pulled out the book he riffled the pages. If I had cut out a hiding place for a small pistol it would have fallen out. The guard had not looked at the book. His eyes were trained on me. He shook the book twice. Nothing happened and he did not look happy. He tipped his beret back an inch and said with sudden menace, "What's the game, sir?"

I waggled my eyebrows and pointed with my chin. "Isn't it your birthday? The guys told me it was your birthday."

"It is not my birthday, sir."

The other guards relaxed visibly and one of them let out a guffaw.

"Aw, that's too bad. We all wrote a birthday wish for you."

The guard looked at the book and then back at me. "I don't get it."

Like Quire said, the book is not for everyone. I felt like a deflating balloon. I was only saved from utter failure when one of the other guards walked up and snatched the book from the first man's hands.

The mind virus took over the second guard as its message shot straight to his big, juicy amygdala.

42

TIRED

I could tell by the way the man's jaw went slack that the book had taken whatever toll was to be paid. He did a slow 360-degree turn to take in the mountain and the view as if he'd never seen it before. When he turned back to me, a goofy smile was smeared across his face. "Thank you!"

"Uh, you're welcome."

The man dropped the book and his rifle to the pavement and started off down the mountain. The head of the security detail called after him, "Blackford! Where in hell do you think you're going?"

"We're all in hell already, friends!" Blackford turned but kept going, walking backward with that same disconcerting smile. "Nice day for a walk, though, ain't it? You know what? I've never been to Iceland! I want to go to Iceland!"

"Get your ass back here and bring the rest of you along with it, you useless piece of shit!"

"Nah, I'm good! I want to see more of everything before it's all at the bottom of a lake of fire. Thanks, though! It's been an experience! Have a nice day!"

The guard who'd been unaffected by the book looked back and

forth from the man going AWOL to me. He nodded to two of the other guards and they went after Blackford. "Since the attack on Wall Street, we're at DEFCON 3. We have a little patience but it is worn thin and microscopic if you read me, sir."

"Roger that."

"We got a call to be on the lookout for you. They said you might be armed and dangerous. The men and I find that hard to believe but, have you got something to tell me, sir? Any weapons on you —
"

"Just trying to save the world."

"Us, too, sir."

"I know. That's the sad part. It's sad that the roles we play have been so necessary."

Blackford was hauled back by the two other guards. Besides dragging his feet, the man did not resist.

One of the men who held Blackford demanded of him, "What is your malfunction, Private?"

The man began to giggle. "I've stood out here, rain or shine, winter and summer. Until this minute, I never thought about how futile it is. It's like we're rakin' leaves at my parents' house. We had so many huge oaks and there was always more to rake. I never really got it all before the snow came. When the fallout comes, best case scenario, we're stuck in a can, man. If we stay here when it all goes down, we are not the lucky ones. Better to be right at ground zero, first to be hit so we won't have to think about it for long."

Blackford began to weep. "When it really goes off, accidentally or on purpose, does anybody really want to be safe behind those blast doors? What does safe even mean? We'd just die slow or eat each other in the end. Suppose we cram a couple hundred people in there and wait it out. Do you really want to be a survivor? It would suck worse than anything you can imagine."

One of the guards holding him demanded, "Why you bawling, Blackford?"

"'Cuz I got a good imagination! Can't you see what's headed right for us? I wanna see some tropical sunsets and more titties before the balloon goes up!"

The guards who had pinned his arms looked at each other and I heard one whisper, "He's cracked." One gripped his shoulder, now in a brotherly way. "It's okay, Jason. It's okay. Let's go in and you can talk to somebody, okay?" The man consoling Blackford turned to the sergeant standing between me and the bus. "Jason is a good man, Sarge. Toughest son of a bitch I know. Happens to the best of us. Gotta be PTSD."

The other guard at Blackford's side let go. "Sorry, Jason. Sucks, man." The mood of the men changed suddenly and they looked contrite for treating their comrade harshly. Then the guard who'd let go of Jason Blackford bent to pluck the book from the ground.

Too late, the sergeant shouted for him to drop it. The man froze for just a moment. I hoped the guard would react as Rhythm Method had and run off on a quest to raise money for Colorado's homeless or something. Instead, he raised his M-16 and shot the man who had been so kind to Blackford.

The wounded man fell to the ground, clutching his chest. As he gasped his last, he didn't look at the gunman. He looked at Blackford and reached up with one hand.

Blackford held the wounded man's hand and patted it gently. "Too late for titties. Y'all got surprised to death. Told you the balloon was gonna go up. It's what balloons do."

The man who had fired his rifle looked down at the fallen man. For a horrible second, I saw a smile cross his face. The initial sudden shock passed through us like an electrical current. Then the sergeant who had stopped me pushed forward as he drew his sidearm. But the rifleman was quick, too. He whirled and almost shot me.

It was Blackford who saved me from getting a new hole in my head. He tackled the shooter and pulled him to the ground. The man who had attempted to walk away from his post continued to weep as he struggled for the weapon. "Enough!" the crying man whispered in the shooter's ear. "Haven't we all had enough? Why can't we figure out how to get along? Why? I bet we could if we really wanted to!"

The staff on the bus were shouting and the driver took off. I wondered if it was Ed, the sergeant who looked so much like Ed

Harris. No more joking around about *Invasion of the Bodysnatchers* with him.

Though the shooter was on his back, the sergeant did not jump in to try to help subdue him. He shot him instead, four rounds to the chest with his XM17 service pistol. The man went limp. Blackford was covered in blood from the dead men on either side of him.

"Get your shit in order and stowed, Blackford!" the sergeant yelled.

Blackford panted as he got to his feet. I thought he had snapped out of it for a moment before he went AWOL again. He staggered at first and then settled into a lackadaisical pace to head down the mountain once more.

"Where do you think you're going?" the sergeant demanded.

I cleared my throat. "I think he said Iceland. And, uh … titties." I didn't mean to be funny but the ridiculousness of my statement hit after I uttered it and I heard Blackford giggle.

The sergeant turned his pistol on me. "I don't know what you're up to but it's no good, is it?"

I stared into the pistol's black mouth. "I worked the cost-benefit analysis. In the big picture, it looks like I'm on the side of the angels."

"Shut up!" His hands were shaking from just having killed one of his own. I could tell, this man was a good soldier. The book hadn't affected him. He had purpose and he believed he was in the right. That's why it hurt me when the spare tire from the back of my Bronco sailed through the air and hit him squarely in the head. He must have been dead before he hit the ground.

I turned to see Quire standing by the entrance to the parking lot. She blessed me with one of her rare smiles. Unaccountably strong, she'd thrown the tire with deadly accuracy and from a great distance. Unfortunately, she was not bulletproof.

I'd forgotten about the fifth guard who had hung back behind the bus. Guarding the far side, he'd stayed in my blind spot, too. He fired his machine gun into Quire. She stood against the hail of bullets, neither falling nor advancing. The soldier stalked forward.

He kept on firing until his magazine was empty, quickly changed mags and continued firing.

Finally, Quire fell dead in the road.

The remaining soldier and I stood frozen for a moment as steam rose over Quire's body. At least, I thought it was steam. Then it was smoke. The body seemed to shrink and flatten as it liquified before our eyes. It wasn't blood that stretched long fingers across the pavement. The thin fluid was bright white. It ran out of her, quick as mercury. What little remained of Quire burst into blue flame.

Astonished, the guard asked, "What the hell was that thing?"

It was the sight of her body emptying out that triggered me. I projectile vomited across the pavement.

The guard looked at his handiwork and began to laugh.

It was his laughter that got to me. Laughter isn't an uncommon battlefield reaction to the unexpected but still, the sound hurt me physically. I reached down. I could have picked up the book and tossed it to the remaining guard. Maybe he would have given it a glance. Perhaps upon reading it he would have run down the mountain on some mission of healing and helping. I didn't pick up the book, though. I felt a pressure in my head and chest, a biological need that demanded to be unleashed. I picked up the sergeant's XM17 and emptied it into the guard. The sergeant had spent four shots on one man. As my vision blurred with tears, I pulled the trigger until it clicked empty.

If I'd used the book, it would have revealed the truth of the guard's character. I could have given him the opportunity to punish himself, to achieve his own justice. He was doing his job, true, but I didn't need the book to know he was a bad person. I was sure. He laughed as he killed Quire and then he laughed at my revulsion. He was enjoying himself too much and I hated him for it. I poured thirteen shots into her killer. I didn't simply want to kill him. I wanted to *erase* him. The power behind the mortal words felt so right. I thought I was interested in justice but this was vengeance and it was nearly orgasmic.

We deserve the book, I thought. *Good and bad people alike, we deserve all of it. There are no good guys and bad. Some have a penchant for violence but we all share the same potential. Let's get judged!*

In that moment of anger, I wanted to mow down every evil person. Jaywalkers wouldn't have been safe. Whatever the book did, it wasn't merely right. It was a joyous divine reciprocation, cause and effect. In other words, karma's a bitch.

As I stood over the man I'd killed, the pressure in my head eased. Conscience slowly returned and then flooded over me. The horror crept back anew and I was drowning.

"Maybe I'm the bad guy now," I gasped. "Good and bad doesn't mean as much as I thought it did. The two aren't as far apart as I thought."

I wondered if I should say something more but all I could come up with was, "Sorry."

The rifleman was far beyond my apology or any chance at redemption. Plagued with doubt and regret, I threw up again and again until there was nothing left to give.

There was nothing left for me to do at the gate. On rubbery legs, I found my way to the guard detail's Jeep and headed into Cheyenne Mountain Complex.

43

FREE WILL, DIVINE OR OTHERWISE

I sped toward the next checkpoint and caught up to the bus. As I screeched to a halt, I narrowly missed running over the security detail as they scattered to get out of my way. The XM17 was empty but no one on the bus knew it. I jumped out of the Jeep as a guard stepped off the bus. I pointed the pistol at him and shoved him aside. I managed to get on the bus before the guards could open fire. I was oddly grateful to find Ed, my usual morning driver, in the driver's seat. "Shut the door, Sergeant!"

Everyone on the bus began shouting at me to put the gun down. Ed seemed to take it in stride. He did as I ordered and closed the door. Then he picked up the mic so his words would punch through the din. "We have a situation. Everybody sit down and calm your tits while I talk to the Lieutenant Colonel. Nobody do anything stupid back there and we won't, either. Thank you."

The world was upside down and it felt good to find a stoic. "Hi, Ed."

"Lt. Col. Salvador? Did the bodysnatchers get you?"

"Something like that."

"Seems so."

No one except Ed was armed. "I'm going to have to relieve you of your sidearm, Ed."

"I imagine you would," he replied. He was old-school, still packing a Beretta M9. He handed it over. "Good plan so far, sir. Somebody will give me a lot of hassle later for not shooting you. If I could shoot you, I'd be obligated. You understand."

I ducked down before the guards outside the bus could line up a shot. "Somebody else will do it soon, I'm sure."

"No worries, then," Ed replied.

I had stumbled into becoming a hostage taker. Many of my hostages were colleagues. I had the empty XM17, Ed's Beretta and, of course, the book that would end the world, or at least kill billions and change it forever. Despite Ed's announcement, many of the passengers were murmuring among themselves. I imagined a plan was forming to rush me. I learned something important about developing a leadership style: Waving a book around does not get anybody to sit down and shut up. Wielding pistols accomplished that task pretty well, though.

That done, I sat on the floor out of the guards' line of fire and told Ed to hand me the mic to the radio. I clicked the mic a couple of times to let the comm center know I had a message. I was still deciding what to say when General Pitmore's voice came through the speaker. "Salvador? That you on my bus?"

What do you say to a boss you hate at the end of the world? Anything you want. "I'd say it's my bus right now, Stewart."

"You will address me as General Pitmore."

"Nah, I don't think so. Things are about to even out, Stewie."

I'd eaten a lot of shit under his command and bottled up a lot of anger. Pitmore valued missiles, warheads and nuclear payloads. Enamored of the power of the split atom and hydrogen yield, he was stuck in a Cold War mentality that wouldn't have been out of place in the last century. He often quoted Truman about how our weapons of mass destruction were "harnessing the basic power of the universe." Since the advent of the internet and cyberwar, I considered him about as relevant as an old warhorse pulling a cannon.

"Salvador? Report!"

I paused, trying to figure out how to describe the power of the book in as few words as possible without sounding insane. "The apocalypse is already underway. It's not your flavor of apocalypse, though. This is kind of like the Rapture, Stewart, but messier than the Rapture. The assholes off themselves for the most part and the good people get to stay on Earth."

I'd managed to state the facts succinctly but I'd missed the mark on sounding sane. I sounded crazier than a three-legged dog in a fire hydrant factory. Even so, I was surprised to find that when Pitmore came back on the radio, he sounded like he believed me. "Are you responsible for the attack on Wall Street?"

"That wasn't me."

"Who did it?"

"There are forces at work. I ran into a couple of people who identified themselves as federal agents. They knew what was going on. Then, in Newport News, some contractors tried to take the … the weapon. They killed my mother in the process. Long story."

"What is the weapon?"

"It's Destruction's delivery system. Think of it as a codebook that unlocks … something dangerous within each of us."

"What's the something exactly? Specifics, Salvador!"

"Our true natures. It works according to the heart of each reader. Let me in and we'll talk about it. I want the meeting in my office, just you and me."

The light background static on the radio stretched out in the chasm between reason and desperation, between the beginning and the end. With too much exposure, white noise becomes torture. Sitting on the floor with a busload of hostages, two guns and the book that would end the world, white noise summed up how I felt about people. People are like white noise: mostly fine in small doses — maybe even calming. With long exposure, people could be torturous, too.

I wiped tears from my eyes as I thought again of the horror of Quire's death and how her body melted in the summer sun. I had not understood that powerful exotic creature. Despite her otherworldliness, I was certain she bore me less malice than General Stewart Pitmore.

My superior came back on the mic. "Intelligence has been working overtime. We have some ideas about what you've got. We want it."

"Of course you do."

"Let my people off the bus and I guarantee you safe passage into the complex. Better in our hands than in the hands of our enemies, don't you agree, Lt. Col. Salvador?"

I shot Ed a grim smile and didn't key the mic right away. I wanted to make him sweat for a change. "Notice he's using my rank again. The General is trying to appeal to my patriotism while stroking his vanity. The general is a prolapsed anus of a human being. Do you think he's aware?"

Ed grinned. "I couldn't say with certainty, sir, but my pop used to say that if you sit in the outhouse too long, you don't smell shit anymore. I suspect General Pitmore does not smell his own shit, no."

"Somebody should tell him," I said.

Ed looked at me earnestly. "This isn't going to end well, is it, sir?"

"Everything's changing, Sergeant. You want to know the real twist?"

"What's that, sir?"

"When Death comes knocking, we're going to *know* we deserve it. Some of us will fight it or be bitter and try to take others with us into the dark. But deep down? Deep down the bastards will *know* it's not just Death coming for us. Justice rides with it."

Ed surprised me by quoting scripture. "'I looked and behold, a white horse! And its rider had a bow and a crown was given to him and he came to conquer.' You from Revelation, sir? Are you the guy on the horse?"

"Nah, I think I'm just the horse. Maybe just the ass. You religious, Ed?"

"A little but not particularly," the sergeant allowed. "I'm just hoping for a better world after this one. I've worked at the mountain that could end the world for half my career. Lots of us at Cheyenne can quote you chapter and verse. I never thought God would take us out, though. We've got whizbangs as tall as buildings and the big red buttons to send them around the planet. Most people have the luxury of not thinking about it, but we've already come close to going up in a mushroom cloud several times. I always figured we'd do it to ourselves, probably by accident."

"This won't be an accident. This will be an act of will, free, divine or otherwise."

The book, tucked under the belt at the small of my back, sent an icy chill up my spine again, hungry for human souls.

44

WHEN A DOOR IS A JAR

Everyone except Ed filed off the bus through the rear exit. The sergeant volunteered to stay with me, as driver and hostage. By their faces, I could tell some of my colleagues left relieved to get out of the field of fire. Most shot me a resentful glare before leaving at gunpoint. They were warriors, after all.

Lt. Havelston had warned me I wasn't socially or politically savvy enough to climb higher on the ladder. I blanked on the first names of several of those staffers so it appeared she was right. If I'd been friendlier, developed more friendships and built trust, I would have had someone else to call for help when the geese got sucked into the jet engine of human existence.

"Sir?"

"Call me Zane"

Ed bobbed his head in agreement. "My father would say you're in a pickle, Zane. My mother would say you're in a fuckle. What's the plan? You don't really think they're going to let you all the way to your office for a solo sit down with the brass, do you?"

"General Pitmore will keep me alive until I hand him what he wants."

"And then?"

"He'll be less polite after that. Mean words and probably summary execution. Unless, of course, they want to torture me for intel — "

"Yeah, they'll definitely want to interrogate, hook you up to a car battery, nipples and nuts."

"Bad hair day all 'round, huh? Well, I guess that's the way of things. Let's go. I gotta get this done." My hands trembled.

Despite Ed's dire warning, I was almost giddy at the prospect of finishing my mission. Quire said I'd get a reward but all I wanted was to find peace and if peace could only come at a high price, I'd make the world pay that price. We hadn't managed to achieve world peace. *Drastic measures are inevitable,* I told myself.

Ed put the bus in gear and we drove into the mountain, under the arch that reads: Cheyenne Mountain Complex. "The Canadians supplied the explosives when they scooped a million tons of dirt out of the mountain. It's one of the Wonders of the World that most will never see. If they court-martial you instead of killing you, think you'll miss us?"

"It's been an honor," I said, "but it's a shame it was necessary. I loved that it was Air Defense. Under Bush, we got into surveillance for the drug war."

"Then 9/11 and counterterrorism," Ed added.

"Operation Noble Eagle," I said. "September 11th was bad, sure, but wait until you see what comes next."

We proceeded down the main tunnel. It was emptied of all personnel. The reason why became clear when we came to the side tunnel that led to Command & Control. The blast door was closed.

"Ed, thanks for the ride. I'll take over. Time for you to head back to the entrance. Tell everybody to stay out. You should all go home for the day."

"I've been driving you to work most days for years. You're one of the few officers that wished me a good morning every damn day. You never said much but you never bothered me, neither. I gotta ask, do you really think you know what you're doing?"

I thought of the hawk-faced man on the train. What was it he told me? *Everything that is about to happen is predestined. It's a script you cannot help but follow.*

"I don't know," I admitted, "but I am sure of one thing: We can't keep going as we are and expect to survive."

Ed surprised me by giving me a sharp salute.

Once the sergeant was out of sight around the curve in the tunnel I picked up the radio mic. "Stewart? It's Zane. If you want the weapon, I need to speak to you face to face."

There was a moment's pause as the General considered my gambit. Then, "You attacked the security detail at the front gate and took hostages, Mr. Salvador. Also, you're armed. I'm not coming on the bus so you can make headlines as a disgruntled employee."

"We both know whatever happens here will be slapped with a label of top secret, Stewart. Open the door so we can chat like gentlemen."

After another moment, my answer came with a long buzzing sound and the *whoop, whoop* of an alarm to let me know the twenty-five ton blast door was opening. It took thirty seconds. That was plenty of time for me to grind the gears on the bus and drive it into the opening.

I parked it in the doorway before it finished opening. My intention was to leave an escape route open, not for me but for the complex's staff. The staff was less concerned for my safety. Before I shut off the engine, I saw several men with M-16s rush to positions to line up a shot.

I threw myself to the floor of the bus again and scrambled for the mic. "Clear those guys out! If I smell even one sniper, I'll destroy the codebook. You want it? Play nice, Stew!"

I settled on to the cold floor, giving them time to retreat before I dared to chance a look. A lot of people don't like their boss. In my estimation, Pitmore was arrogant, dismissive and willfully ignorant of anything that didn't interest him. Making him read from the book would be every put-upon worker's dream come true. Quire said it wasn't up to me to judge but how could I not? To err is human but judging people for erring is human, too. I wouldn't expect Quire to understand. She wasn't one of us. I wasn't certain what she had been.

The radio crackled. "Mr. Salvador. I'm going to need you to come out of that bus with your hands up. Cooperate. It'll go easier on you."

"Easier? A quick execution with a couple shots to the head instead of sending me to Guantanamo?"

I gasped as I heard the long buzz and the *whoop, whoop* of the door alarm again. I had my answer. The blast door began to close on the bus.

45

WALLS CLOSE IN

Metal squealed, crumpled and crunched. The small bus rocked and shivered. The windows burst first with loud bangs, eight times, one after another. I'd parked the vehicle only part way through the small opening. I assumed the huge door would crush the bus like a soda can. Instead, it began to break through, cutting the bus apart just behind me. The door was an unrelenting jaw and the bus might as well have been cotton candy.

As the vehicle twisted in the grip of the twenty-five ton door, the windshield crinkled as its frame broke. The snipers were waiting for me to pop my head up for a clear shot. There was no way forward or back.

Trapped and desperate, I clutched the paperback to my chest. On my journey to Cheyenne, blood had spattered its battered cover. Its spine was broken and some of the edges of its pages had been singed. At this range, the Beretta was useless against rifles. The book was the only effective weapon I had in my arsenal.

Each weapon's lethal potential repels some. Lethality attracts many, though. We want to hold the power of life and death in our hands. I'd observed this property before. It is evident in any instrument of death. Whether dropped in dirt or covered in dust, a mysterious signal reaches out from *any* weapon.

This dark influence touches something elemental in many humans. The first caveman who picked up a rock to turn a rival's head to paste felt the call. Cain probably used a stone in the first murder. The jawbone of an ass proved handy for Samson to kill a thousand Philistines. Fables all, of course, but weapons spoke to the human condition long before words came along. Weapons meant survival.

The rush of the kill and love of death's instruments were probably rooted in an ancestral yearning for meat from the hunt. Later, maybe the visceral need sprang from an undeniable ache for safety at home or domination in war. Power, like love, sends an unspoken demand to be exercised. You can see this effect at any firing range, gun show or on the battlefield. We care for our weapons, guard them as jealously as a young lover. We even name them. At its worst, the impulse to use a weapon expresses a dirty hope to feel like a vengeful God.

Against my pounding heart, the paperback felt ice cold. I didn't understand how I could know, but I felt the weapon's need. The book was hungry for more blood.

Then I remembered it could be more than a weapon. Careful to avoid looking at the text of any page, I bent the book again so I could only see the page numbers. I stopped at page 124 to use the book's most banal and benign capacity. The strange lullaby wouldn't work on everyone but it was the morning after a long night shift. Surely at least some of the graveyard shift's skeleton crew were tired and wanted to go home to bed. I clicked the radio mic. What little that was left of the bus was being ground against the doorframe but the radio worked on a separate battery and worked fine.

Curled up in a ball, I depressed the transmit button and read the strange poem that had put me so deeply asleep. I didn't let go until I finished with, "Breathe for the world and listen to the gentle fall of snow ... on snow, snow ... on snow."

Somewhere in the cavernous environs of Cheyenne Mountain, the sound of clatters and thunks reached me. I was pretty sure that was the sound of rifles hitting the floor followed by bodies.

Sweet music.

IN THE MOUTH OF MADNESS

"Salvador?" General Pitmore sounded pissed. I wasn't happy about that. I wanted to hear his fear, not irritation.

"Yes, Stewart?"

"What are you playing at?"

"How many people fell asleep?"

"Twelve. They won't wake up. You put them in a coma!"

"They'll be fine. I had the deepest sleep I ever had after reading that little passage. Shift work is brutal on the body and mind. They'll wake up eventually," I said.

"What was the point of that?"

"A demonstration. Would you like a not-so-nice demo? Shall I read something more deadly?"

I was bluffing. To spread the word to the world, I needed to get to the Comm Center. Reading more from the book at that moment could lead to chaos and more gunfire directed my way. However, my gamble paid off. "What do you want, Salvador?" Pitmore asked.

"Pull the snipers back. I'll come out and you come out. We'll have a peaceful conversation. No tricks."

I was just buying time, trying to get out of the crosshairs. I didn't really have a plan except I needed to get to the third floor of

Building C. There were fifteen buildings in the complex. I had to get to the communications node in the command center next to my office. From there, I could broadcast the codes that would unleash the Reverse Rapture.

"Alright, you truculent son of a bitch," Pitmore responded. "For my safety, I will bring one armed escort."

"I'm armed, you're armed. Whatever. I gotta pee so let's get this over with."

I heard the order go out for the snipers to pull back. Noises echo in the chamber so the running feet sounded like a whole platoon. When I peeked out I saw two men with rifles slung over their shoulders. They'd hooked an unconscious man under his arms and, between them, dragged him toward the Satellite Surveillance Node. The sight could have been disturbing but instead, it was comical. The unconscious man snored so loudly, I thought of a buzz saw.

A few minutes later Pitmore strode into view with his aide, Lt. Megan Havelston, trailing behind. He held a pistol. Megan was unarmed. I pointed the Beretta at Pitmore. He kept coming until I told him to stop a few paces from the front of the ruined bus. "Good morning, Stew. Hi, Megan."

Pitmore sneered at me. "You're a traitor to your country and your oath."

"Pleasant as ever, Stewart."

"He's not wrong, Zane," Megan said. "This is not what I'd expect from you."

The look on her face hurt me more than all of Pitmore's bluster. I'd disappointed her. I hadn't expected this of me, either. But she hadn't seen what I'd seen in the last few days, either. "The trouble we've got is bigger than one country, I'm afraid."

"Lt. Havelston informs me that you have some personal animus toward me."

"I don't think you like me much, either."

He nodded. "Never did. You give the impression of a man who thinks he's better than others, who knows what's best for everybody else. I'm sure you think you're better than me."

"And you don't?"

"I'm a general. Knowing what's best for others is my job."

"You're not good at that," I replied.

I'd felt the hunger for blood from the book. At that moment, I felt a powerful urge coming from the weight of the Beretta in my palm. "For everyone's sake, we all better hope I have better judgment than you."

"Twelve of my people seem to be asleep and we can't rouse them. You've got an interesting parlor trick there, yeah, but I've been to Vegas. I've seen some pretty impressive magic shows. What's the game? Did you induce mass hysteria somehow? You get someone to poison Cheyenne's spring with LSD or a slow-acting sedative or something?"

"It's the book. Just the book."

"Before I take this up the chain, I'm going to need another demonstration," Pitmore said.

"Take a look at the surveillance footage from the front gate."

"We did. Inconclusive. I see a bunch of my men going crazy. We've experimented with gaseous tech to induce psychosis. You're telling me a few hypnotic words can cook up murder — "

"Not hypnosis exactly but murder and murder-suicide, yes. For others, the effect is different. One of the guards at Checkpoint Alpha ... Blackford, Jason Blackford. He got an epiphany that made him want to go tour more of the world and live a little larger." I left out the bit about wanting to see more breasts.

"You understand our skepticism, though," Megan said. "We need it explained. We need to examine and test it. That's what we do with dangerous weapons — "

"I gave you a demonstration and it was enough to get you to come out here."

"Quibble, squabble, malarkey and argle-bargle!" Pitmore boomed.

"You kiss your mother with that mouth, Stewart?"

Megan stepped in front of the General. "Zane, please put down the gun. This isn't you."

"Didn't use to be. Then one of my best friends killed himself. That left my other best friend a widow and single mother. Then I saw my own mother murdered in front of me by guys like you, Pitmore. There are people who are out to get hold of the book and use it for their own purposes. I'm told that's not what it's for — "

Megan took another step closer. "You've isolated yourself. I think you're lonely and you need help. Someone is using you — "

"I've been eating shit for a long time. You never get used to the taste."

The lieutenant's gaze held mine and when the burning words reached her, I sincerely hoped the power of the book would spare her. She was one of the good humans. "This world is put together badly, Megan. Life's a woodchipper. We're the wood. If a strategic strike can save us, my way is better than his. We're a big ball of arguments and the hate is escalating. There's going to be a blow-up and it's going to get ugly. What I do today might save us from a civil war tomorrow."

"You can't know that."

"I have it on good authority."

"Philosophy 101, Zane. What is the appeal to authority?"

A common fallacy and terrible logic. You have me there, I thought.

"The book can heal people, too. I've seen it. I know it looks crazy from the outside but I've got to do this." I didn't sound as confident as I should.

"If the book is all you say it is, you're giving up on people. Whatever you've gone through, I'm sorry. I'm sorry about your mother. But — "

"I'm like the Blues Brothers," I said. "I'm on a mission from God." It had always cracked me up how Dan Aykroyd delivered that line in the movie. He didn't say *god* or *gawd*. He said, *gad*.

"They'll kill you," Megan said.

"That happens with everybody on a mission from God, doesn't it? I'm going to do what you're supposed to do when there's about to be a big fight, Megan. I'm going to use my words."

It was Pitmore who settled the argument. He stepped behind Megan and pointed his pistol at her head. "Toss out the book, Salvador. Give it to me. I want to read it."

He'd found his wedge. I didn't want Megan's brains splattered everywhere. She didn't deserve that and I did want Stewart Pitmore to read the mortal words. I didn't hesitate to throw the paperback to him.

He caught it deftly. His smug smile felt like a sharp slap across my face.

"Go ahead, Stewart. Might be the first book you've read in years."

He did not open the paperback. He didn't even glance at the cover. "I'm not altogether convinced, Salvador. I still think you're probably crazy and full of old rope. You've always had a little too much of what the cat licks his ass with. Still, I don't want to be made the fool. I wouldn't sit in the front row of a magic show, either."

To my horror, he handed the book to Megan. "Enjoy some light reading, Lieutenant. Before I hand over a book of magic spells to my superiors, I need to see more of what it can do. I am not taking the word of a psychotic traitor. I need to see for myself from a trust-worthy officer."

Megan was blinking hard, frightened. "Sir?"

"That's an order, Lieutenant." He still used her as a shield, still pointed his pistol at her skull. We store many of the important bits in our skulls. I was frightened for her.

"Don't!" In the tight quarters of the wrecked bus, I tried to scrabble to my left to get a clear shot at Pitmore.

Too late.

Megan opened the book and began to read the words that had already triggered so many deaths. Nothing happened. She flipped forward a few pages and read some more. She chuckled a little, then laughed harder. When that wave ebbed she looked up at me, puzzled and bemused. "Oppenheimer and burning paintings? Really?"

"You know about that? That's in there?"

"Have you even read this, Zane?"

"I've, uh, minimized my exposure," I admitted. "I read a few phrases that sounded like gibberish on the train and the lullaby that puts people to sleep. Besides that — "

"What's so funny, Lieutenant?" Pitmore demanded.

She ignored him and held the book out to me. She flipped through blank pages from the back of the paperback. When Megan hit text, she smiled as she showed me the page.

My jaw dropped as I read the loop:

"I've, uh, minimized my exposure," I admitted. "I read a few phrases that sounded like gibberish on the train and the lullaby that puts people to sleep. Besides that — "

"What's so funny, Lieutenant?" Pitmore demanded.

"Whoa," I said. "Meta."

And on the page, the words appeared:

"Whoa," I said. "Meta."

47

YOU KNOW WHAT THIS MEANS?

You are still reading this book and yet, presumably, you haven't
killed yourself or anyone else. If so, you may count yourself among
the designated survivors of the mortal words.
Congratulations!

Does your safety make you feel at all different
about whether others should be eliminated from Earth's equation?

In any case, you are here for a reason. If you have not done so
already, find that reason.
That is my task, as well.

48

STRANGE LOVE

"Neat trick!" Megan said.

I lowered the Beretta and stared at the book, hopelessly confused. "How is this happening?"

"If you don't know, who does, Zane?"

"The only person I could ask is dead. And she wasn't really a person."

Fed up, Pitmore pushed the lieutenant aside and snatched the book from my hands. He pointed his pistol at me. I dropped the Beretta to the floor of the bus. "That's more like it," he said. "I told you I'd seen magic acts in Vegas. There's always a logical explanation. You better start telling me what that explanation is or I will perforate you repeatedly, Salvador."

"Ed's mom was right."

"Huh?"

"I'm in a fuckle," I said.

"Enough!" General Pitmore glanced at the book. I watched his eyes tracking back and forth, back and forth. He flipped a page, scanned it and flipped to the next and the next. Slowly, the beginnings of a grin began to tug at the corners of his mouth. Then he began to laugh just as Megan did.

I took a deep breath, held it and let out a long sigh. If the book couldn't take Pitmore out of life's unbalanced equation, it seemed the mortal words were out of power. If so, what had all this suffering been for? How much of all that had happened to me was a con? Was it all a sick hallucination?

But the book was not out of power.

Pitmore began to laugh harder and harder. It climbed from an angry maniacal laugh to a hysterical trill. I expected him to shoot me in the head or order his aide to take me prisoner. Instead, he spun on his heel and stalked back toward the Missile Command Node. "I get it now, Zane!"

"What?"

"It's time to get this party started! We've already waited too long. We should have attacked when we were the only ones who had the tech! Doesn't matter! We'll wipe 'em all out now! It's going to be beautiful! Picture it! Deserts of glass! We'll burn them down and begin again! It all makes so much sense now!"

"General! Wait! Stop!"

Megan hurried after him. "General! What are you thinking?"

"I see it all like I'm looking down from space! I feel like the hero of a movie! The answer to all our problems was inside me the whole time!" He couldn't stop laughing.

Megan broke protocol and put a hand on his shoulder to stop him. "Sir! You can't do this!"

"Nonsense, Lieutenant! In case of attack, commanders of nuclear arms have the authority to launch attacks. That's been the case since President Kennedy! I don't need the Commander-in-Chief to start World War III. Talk about the element of surprise! We're going to surprise our own, too! Our enemies got us with Pearl Harbor and 9/11. It amazes me it hasn't occurred to me to do this until now. I was holding back! I feel so clear. We're not just going to clear the board. We're going to flip the board over!"

"They'll shoot you, General," Megan warned.

"After I've pushed the button and saved the world, perhaps. Maybe they'll thank me. Doesn't matter. I just figured out how little anything matters." Pitmore lashed out with his pistol and hit Megan across the face. She rocked to one side and almost lost her balance. Her hands went to her jaw. She spat blood and two teeth to the ground. He lashed out again and this time she collapsed.

I scooped up the Beretta and climbed out of the front of the bus where the windshield had been. "Pitmore!"

He paused to look back and smile. His eyes were huge and crazy, his brow shiny with sweat. "Thank you, Zane. I've been contemplating this eventuality for years. The funny thing is, once you let go of your part in the story of your life, you see things objectively. I got my head screwed on right."

"No, sir. You're under the influence of the book! There are … " I searched for an explanation. "There are psychedelic compounds in the pages!"

"Nah," he said. "That doesn't seem likely. You see, Zane, I'm on a mission from God."

He didn't say it in the funny way Dan Aykroyd had delivered the line in *The Blues Brothers*. He said it with the over-the-top delivery George C. Scott uttered in *Dr. Strangelove*. Everyone who worked at Cheyenne had watched *How I Learned to Stop Worrying and Love the Bomb*. The movie was required watching, in high rotation on the screens in the complex's gym and a staple of the night shift every Halloween.

"So," the General said. "You brought the apocalypse. Are you with me? Want a front-row seat to the end of tyranny and the rise of a new world?"

"It won't be like a phoenix from the ashes, General," Megan said. "It'll be extermination."

"Death all around! You want world peace! There's only one way to world peace!" Pitmore enthused. "Annihilation!"

When I closed my eyes, I saw people throwing themselves from burning towers, falling through poisoned smoke. "I've seen this movie. I know how it ends."

I was an agent of the coming apocalypse but I wasn't going to be the catalyst for Pitmore's nuclear version. Nukes are not discerning weapons. Knowing the kind of man he was, I didn't feel any sharp pangs of remorse, only dull ones. Pitmore simply wasn't a good enough man to bother with tears. I chose to focus on that fact as I stopped the world from being erased.

I shot General Stewart Pitmore through the chest several times. Ironically enough, it was execution for the highest treason. His was not a betrayal to one flag. He'd been about to betray them all.

49

THE SOCIAL INFECTION

Armed with the book and a few rounds left in the Beretta, I sprinted for Building C. Megan called after me. I ignored her and kept going. I thought I'd finally caught a break when I saw a guard on the other side of the door flat on the floor. He was curled up in the fetal position and sleeping peacefully. One less obstacle to worry about.

Fumbling for my badge, I zipped it through the scanner. To my horror, the keycard code had been changed. My mission was at a dead end. I looked around, searching for another way to the Comm Node. After all I'd endured to come this far, I couldn't imagine that I'd be stopped cold by one locked door.

The solution arrived in the form of another problem. "Step back from the door or I'll blow your head off — "

I whirled and fired without aiming. Gutshot, the airman went down hard. Writhing in pain, he managed to squeeze off one round. The bullet tore through my left shoulder. The force of it spun me and I dropped the Beretta as I sank to the deck.

Lying beside him, we both moaned in pain. I recognized the airman. He worked in Building C just down the hall from my office.

Matthew Foreman was a soft-spoken young man, barely past the legal age to drink.

Foreman looked at me, wide-eyed and going into shock. I suppose I was, too.

"It's not like the movies, is it, sir?" He coughed and winced in more pain as he did so. "Both shot, nobody wins."

"Sorry, Matthew. Can't explain what has to be done. I'm told it's going to be worth it."

I crawled to him, pulled his lanyard over his head and snatched up the Beretta.

"What was that thing?" Foreman asked.

"What thing?"

"On the surveillance recording," he said. "Threw a tire like it was nothing." The airman began to pant rapidly, desperately trying to catch his breath.

I screamed for a medic even as I got to my feet to abandon him. "Save your energy and hold on, Matthew. Help'll be here in a second."

"But what was that thing?"

The truth was that I wasn't sure. I assumed I was on the side of the angels but as I looked down at the young man I'd shot, doubt crept in. I didn't have time to think about it. I was committed and couldn't imagine changing course.

The entry code on my card no longer worked but Matthew Foreman's badge did.

My left arm hung loose and pain knifed through my shoulder as I struggled to keep going before I bled out. Mercifully, the lock buzzed.

"Zane!"

I looked back to find Megan staggering toward me. Her face was covered in blood and she held one hand over her forehead to stanch the flow of blood. "What are you doing?"

"What needs to be done." I nodded toward Foreman. "Put pressure on that wound!"

When the lieutenant took her hand away from her forehead I saw the source of the blood running down her face. Pitmore had opened a wound across the width of her forehead. She would survive and get stitches but unless she got emergency plastic surgery soon, Megan would probably wear her hair in bangs for the rest of her life.

"I'm sorry this is necessary."

"But is it, Zane?"

I closed the door behind me and hurried as fast as I could to the stairs. The staircase to the third floor was a regular part of my cardio program. I prided myself on taking the steps two at a time. For my last day at Cheyenne, that wasn't an option. I leaned my right shoulder against the wall and pulled myself along with my right hand. A trail of blood followed me up the stairs. The average adult body contains about one and a half gallons of blood, but we can only stand to lose forty percent of it before dropping dead. Time was running out on my blood clock.

On the second floor, I glimpsed three of my staff. They must have assumed I was armed because they ran to the far stairwell to get to an exit. More guards would arrive soon. I was pretty sure the Beretta was empty or close to it. I spent one round on poor Airman Foreman but I hadn't counted my shots when I took Pitmore down. When the guards decided to storm Building C, they'd kill me easily if I didn't fall to blood loss first.

Breathing heavily and feeling weak, I made it to the third floor and stumbled to Cheyenne Mountain's Comm Node for the National Civilian Signaling System. I locked the steel door behind me. That wouldn't stop my pursuers but it would slow them.

Most people are familiar with the Amber Alert System, the warning that is broadcast widely when a child is abducted. The NCSS is an Amber Alert to the tenth power. The bulletin I sent would interrupt radio and television broadcasts as well as beam into cell phones in Canada, the United States, Mexico and all our NATO allies across the world.

US Pacific Command had caused quite a stir on January 13, 2018 when a false alarm was sent out to every resident in Hawaii. A technician had clicked his mouse on the wrong option and the pants-shitting signal had gone out:

. . .

BALLISTIC MISSILE THREAT INBOUND TO HAWAII. SEEK IMMEDIATE SHELTER. THIS IS NOT A DRILL.

I DROPPED into a chair and slapped the paperback on the table. I picked up a pad with my good arm. From here, the signal would be routed through USNORTHCOM and beamed just about everywhere. No matter what happened next, I'd be dead soon. I didn't think about what I would miss. I'd never see Charlotte and Alek's baby. I'd never see that baby grow up.

But mostly, I pondered the things I had already missed. I thought again of Jocelyn and how different my life might have been had I invited her into my dorm on that fateful sunny afternoon. Or was it more accurate to call it fateless?

On the premise of condemning a huge chunk of the world's population, Jocelyn's argument came back to me: *Most people are only doing the best they can with what they've got. If you're half as smart as you think you are, help them and educate them. Good people try again. I love* tikkun olam. *It means to aspire to repair the world, to be benevolent in all aspects of your life.*

Quire's view of humanity was much darker. If she was right and basically half of us really were against the other half, we were all doomed, anyway.

"Zane?" It was the intercom by the door.

I turned to find Megan standing in the hallway on the other side of the locked door. Through the narrow window, I could see she held a rifle. I pressed the intercom button on the desk. "Come to say goodbye?"

"They're working on Foreman downstairs. They think he'll make it."

"Good."

"That depends on what you do next."

"About to bless the world with an enema. It's a shitty process, but in the end it should be quite relieving. The comments on

YouTube are about to get a lot more kind."

"If it's as bad as you say, can't you just block the trolls? You don't have to kill them. Ignore 'em and carry on! There aren't that many bad people in the world. Mostly they're just scared. Fear makes them stupid — "

"For a minority, they're awfully loud."

"Even if they're wrong and you're right, most shitty people aren't worth murdering. If you're so much better than them, then be better. Don't become them."

Despite the pain ripping through my shoulder, a low chuckle burst out of me. "I'm not so sure I'm better anymore."

"Then what's so funny?"

"You remind me of someone. A girl in college told me I was too cynical. Working here amps up the paranoia. I think I've ingested too much hate. I thought I was just reading it and thinking about it. I absorbed a lot of it, too. Trolls, bad news and constant threats … it's a social disease. I got the infection aurally."

Megan didn't laugh. Too bad. I'd hoped to go out with a laugh and a bang.

"What are you going to do, Zane?"

"How long do I have?"

"They're coming. I hear them on the stairs."

"Long enough to save the world."

She raised the rifle. "Don't!"

"Don't worry. You've convinced me. The revolution will not be televised. This whole thing only felt right when I was angry, not when I was thinking."

I picked up the pad and typed out a short message before the lieutenant shot me through the glass in the door. It wasn't bullet-proof, just bullet-resistant. It took Megan two mags before her shots began to reach me.

I was much less bullet-resistant but I had just enough time to send out one data blast.

50

RISK TOLERANCE

Shot, dead and gone … or so I thought. I awoke in a cold place. My head throbbed but my shoulder seemed okay. I tried to move my arm and found I couldn't.

Restraints, I thought. *Will they court-martial me or just go straight to the execution? If so, why heal me?*

Ed had warned me: They'll definitely want to interrogate, hook you up to a car battery, nipples and nuts. I shuddered at the thought. I tried to look around but it was as if I was pinned under a great weight. A tube was down my throat and it was uncomfortable. I could not scream for help or even talk. All I could do was hum and that didn't seem very helpful.

Bleary, I struggled to focus. I was in a strange room hooked up to what I took to be medical devices. The room was all metal, too. I lay naked and shivering on a metal slab. The cold seemed to pass through me like a punishing arctic wind.

A voice that seemed to be everywhere and nowhere called my name. "Lieutenant Colonel Salvador. Welcome back."

Hello? I thought. *If this is Hell, can you turn up the heat?*

"I can understand your engrams, Zane."

My what?

235

"I can understand you. What I don't understand is your choice. Was it an impulse in the moment? When you sent the message, how did you make your choice?"

I was just doing the best I could under the circumstances. I wanted to make Jocelyn proud.

After what seemed like a long pause, the voice came again. "So it was your memory of Jocelyn that made you alter the plan? Explain further."

My thoughts were a jumble. My choice was not based on one factoid. I had changed course for a bunch of reasons. Mostly, I think it was Airman Matthew Foreman's question. He asked what Quire was.

I had been an atheist all my life but when trouble came, I desperately wanted to believe I was on the side of angels. Everybody wants to think they're the good guy and never wrong. My trip east had prepared me to trust in Quire. The book had power and the weapon felt right and righteous in my hand. Airman Foreman had not been groomed to believe Quire had wings ready to sprout. He saw what happened and took it for what it was: an attack by a hostile force.

The clues were there all along. I didn't see it because I didn't want to.

"I understand, Zane," the voice said.

I heard the sound of metal sliding against metal somewhere behind me. I tried to crane my neck to see my captor but my skull was clamped tight. I couldn't move my head an inch. Warm hands slipped over my bare shoulders and stayed there for a moment. Heat seeped into me. I felt fear but a comfort, too.

"I promised you ... what did you call it? An after-action report? A debriefing?"

Quire?

"At a few minutes past nine on a lovely summer day in Colorado, your message went out across North America and a good portion of the world. Before the lieutenant killed you, you managed to send one message."

. . .

MESSAGES ON SCREENS ARE CAUSING THE SUICIDAL
IDEATION AND HOMICIDAL IMPULSES YOU'VE SEEN IN
MEDIA. FIGHT ENEMY INFLUENCE. DESTROY COMM
NETWORKS AND YOUR DEVICES IMMEDIATELY. THIS IS
NOT A DRILL.

Did it work?

"There was a high probability no one would believe your warning. However, the pope and cardinals' group suicide flipped those odds."

So religion saved the world, after all?

"You could say that but it would not be wholly accurate."

It would be holy accurate.

"Humor, Zane?"

I guess not.

"Where did the mission go wrong? You are a tactician, Zane. Tell me."

The book has the power to benefit us. It healed Reggie of his limp, eased June's pain and turned a sneaker hoarder into a philanthropist. Demonstrate the helping potential instead of the book's killing potential. Do that and we can have peace.

"We debated that strategy," Quire replied. "It is more probable that dominant countries will fight to keep the power of the book to themselves and attempt to monetize it. Humans are a transactional and territorial species — "

You're no angel, are you?

"No."

Why did you try to make an atheist believe he was on a mission from God?

"The balance of probabilities. As a member of the military, the calculation was that you were more likely to accept a divine authority. Please excuse the deception but if I'd told you we were an invading force, you would have done your duty to alert your superiors. They would have launched a counterattack immediately."

What do you want, Quire?

"Peaceful coexistence."

237

Peace by getting us to kill ourselves and each other? Softening us up for invasion?

"Not invasion, Zane. Immigration is our goal. Eliminating your most toxic citizens increases the likelihood of accepting us, of integration — "

What are you, really?

"You already suspect — "

Tell me!

"An alien species. We are few. When we began our journey, we were many. There are only several hundred of us left. We are in high orbit, waiting for you to make our arrival a safe one."

Then show us what you can build instead of destroying! If you want acceptance, try again and give the good the book can do. Inspire us. Give us hope. Good people try again! Do that and I will welcome our new alien overlords.

As Quire withdrew her hands from my bare shoulders, I noticed she had more than five fingers on each hand. For a brief moment, I saw her at the edge of my vision. She did not look like a pretty young Asian woman. The alien had two huge eyes. The creature's gray skin was rough and the head appeared to be covered in dark thorns. Clothed in black, some kind of large, ungainly-looking device was attached to its left arm and tubes fed into the upper arm. I shuddered at the sight. It was easy to imagine this being walking out of a flying saucer and immediately being met by gunfire.

"Thank you for your efforts, Zane," she said. "I apologize for our deceptions but it was deemed necessary. I assure you, we will weigh your words. We will have to decide quickly. You have been gone too long and we have to send you back."

I don't understand.

"We tapped into your metacognitive loop to explore likely outcomes, to prepare you."

"I followed the script on the holodeck!"

"I understand the metaphor. Yes, the simulation you have experienced is our second attempt to prepare you for the mission. The first attempt was successful in instilling what was at stake — "

I remember. People threw themselves from burning buildings. I was running through some kind of fog and ... someone stole a can of soup from my pack when I was underground.

"The first simulation ended in nuclear annihilation for your species and ours, yes."

War-games. This has all been war-games! You want Heaven on Earth? Invasion and war are not the way to go!

"Our next attempt will be real and it will be our last attempt. There is much trepidation about leaving the fate of two species to the whims of one lone human. There are too many variables. The consensus is that to achieve our goals, you must be weaponized."

Then do as I say and be honest with us. If you want to win us over, use the magic words to help us, don't kill us! There are no necessary dead!

"The collective doubts that strategy will be fruitful but I will present your case."

I've got one more for you, Quire. It's a human magic word. Please!

"Thank you, Zane. Before we return you, your reward ..."

51

AFTER THE EQUALS SIGN

I stood before a blue door. To my right, the telephone sat on the desk. My barbell was on the floor to my left. Someone knocked on the door. I smiled as I rushed to open it.

Jocelyn stood before me just as she'd been in college. I'd forgotten how red her lipstick was that day. I wanted some. Before she could say anything, I opened the door wide and offered my hand. She took it and I pulled her into my dorm room.

Jocelyn laughed. "Hi! What's gotten into you?"

"A higher tolerance for risk, maybe?"

"Weirdo."

"You're not wrong. Sorry, I've been a dick. This is new to me, let's try again. I was an idiot about you dating my buddy before I got the chance. I'm not any more secure than I was about that, but you're worth getting my heart broken."

"Who says you'll get your heart broken?"

"It could happen," I replied, "but that would be better than never knowing you."

She kissed me. I kissed her back. We took our time. She laughed as she broke away to pull me down to the narrow bed. I liked the sound of her laughter. I wanted to give her more reasons to laugh.

"You seem so different," she said.

"I thought about what you said. I've been very attached to being right about everything all the time. It's exhausting. I want to make more room to be happy, too. And I want you, in this room, now."

"Where have you been all my life?" she teased.

"Waiting for you, Jocelyn."

And for a time, there was Heaven on Earth.

52

GENESIS

United States Air Force Lieutenant Colonel Zane Salvador woke up on a night train bound for Chicago. A hawk-faced stranger sat beside him. The slouching man carried a book and nothing more.

The train ate rails and shat miles, plowing through the darkness toward dawn and an uncertain future.

THANK YOU FOR READING AMID MORTAL WORDS!

Authors and their books live and die by reviews. If you dig what I sling, please take a moment to spread the happy word and leave a review wherever you purchased this novel.

You've reached the end of this reading journey but there are many others. After you've left a review, please turn the page for your next escape from reality. As the hawk-faced man said, "A day without reading is a day that is not done."

Cheers and all the best,

Robert

ACKNOWLEDGMENTS

Many thanks to my editor, Gari Strawn of strawnediting.com and my excellent beta reader, Russ Sawatsky. I would also like to thank the members of the inner sanctum on my Facebook fan page. During my recent illness, your words of encouragement helped me persevere. You're super readers and good people.

ABOUT THE AUTHOR

Robert Chazz Chute is a former journalist, speechwriter, book doctor and an award-winning writer living in Other London. He pens killer crime thrillers, suspense and epic apocalyptic science fiction. To find out more about his work, please visit his author page at AllThatChazz.com.*

***If you really love Robert Chazz Chute's work and want even more interaction,
join us on the Facebook fan page (Fans of Robert Chazz Chute) for daily updates and chat.**

facebook.com/robert.c.chute

twitter.com/RChazzChute

instagram.com/robertchazzchute

ALSO BY ROBERT CHAZZ CHUTE

~ DYSTOPIAN & APOCALYPTIC FICTION ~

This Plague of Days, Season 1
This Plague of Days, Season 2
This Plague of Days, Season 3
This Plague of Days, Omnibus Edition

AFTER Life: Inferno
AFTER Life: Purgatory
AFTER Life: Paradise
AFTER Life Box Set

Machines Dream of Metal Gods
(**First in the** *Robot Planet Series,*
only 99 cents!)

Robot Planet, The Complete Series

All Empires Fall: Signals from the Apocalypse
(**anthology**)

THE DIMENSION WAR SERIES

Haunting Lessons
Death Lessons
Fierce Lessons
Dream's Dark Flight

~ TIME TRAVEL ~

Wallflower

~ THE CRIME THRILLERS ~

Bigger Than Jesus

Higher Than Jesus

Hollywood Jesus

Brooklyn in the Mean Time

The Night Man

∾

Coming soon:

Resurrection, **the next book in the** *Hit Man Series*

~ COLLECTIONS ~

Murders Among Dead Trees

Self-help for Stoners

~ NON-FICTION ~

Do the Thing

The Last Stress-busting Book You'll Ever Need

Made in the USA
Middletown, DE
21 March 2020